T0147966

Old Men's Feet

Harold Sparks

iUniverse, Inc.
Bloomington

Old Men's Feet

iUniverse books may be ordered through booksellers or by contacting:

iUniverse
1663 Liberty Drive
Bloomington, IN 47403
www.iuniverse.com
1-800-Authors (1-800-288-4677)

ISBN: 978-1-4759-6819-4 (sc)
ISBN: 978-1-4759-6821-7 (hc)
ISBN: 978-1-4759-6820-0 (e)

Printed in the United States of America

iUniverse rev. date: 5/18/2016

To my Lord and personal savior, Jesus Christ, without whom nothing written here would be possible. I owe you my life and all that I have, for in and of my own accord, I have yet to accomplish anything meaningful during my entire life. All that I have, had, or will have is but a gift from you. Thank you for everything.

$\mathcal{O}ne$

AS THE SUN BEAT DOWN, I pressed onward, but not without pausing to take it all in—the blue and turquoise sea stretching to the horizon, the sound of the waves lapping the shore, the pungent but amiable smell of saltwater. The sun illuminated the perfectly blue sky, and over the sound of wind and waves, I heard birds filling the air with music. The shoreline sounds almost drowned out the noise of technology behind me.

And then there was the air. Ah, yes, the smell of salt permeated everything as the warm breeze blew the odor in from the sea! I stood frozen—relaxed but quietly still, trying to take it all in. I didn't want to miss a moment! I remained, baking in the sun for hours (or maybe moments), trying to make the glorious sensation last.

Somehow, it made me feel alive. I hadn't felt that way since ... not since my wife was with me. She left me alone some time back. Perhaps not willingly, but nevertheless, I was just as alone.

Time had been my friend. It left me alone, for the most part. In fact, some said it had passed me by altogether. My kids sure told me that. Was I really an antique—just a relic from some past world that had faded away? Perhaps my kind had become extinct, almost. There seemed to be fewer and fewer of us around. You know, those old dinosaurs clinging to the old ways. I had been slow to embrace the new technology. Perhaps I had been unwilling to accept it at all.

I cling to the memories of a simpler time—a time when character was respected and people had to have a good work ethic to survive. Now it seems like everybody wants something for nothing. I was always taught that "anything worth having is worth working for" and "there ain't no free ride" and "any job worth doing is worth doing right." Those old clichés seem like lost phrases, like hieroglyphics on some ancient pyramid wall, waiting to be deciphered a thousand years later.

"Excuse me," a young lady called out as she hurried down toward the water. I couldn't help but notice her bathing suit. Now, bathing suits have gone from ordinary bikinis to thongs that barely cover anything. It's not that the female form is unattractive; it's just that displaying so much of it so openly seemed out of place on a lady leading two kids. I guess that's something else I have just been slow to "catch on to."

I realized I had been standing there, in the way. A little embarrassed, I shuffled on behind her, closing in on the beach. As I reached the magical bottom step, civilization ended and the beach began. I stepped off that last remnant of some human manifestation—of manmade civilization—and felt the uneasy movement of the sand below my shoes.

I wore these great beach shoes. I found them at a dollar store. They were more than a dollar but still awfully cheap for a pair of shoes. I figured they were imported shoes of such poor quality they might tear up the first time I wore them. To my surprise—and delight, I might add—they had lasted for several years. The soles were cheap rubber, and the rest of the shoes seemed to be a type of nylon mesh. They were slip-ons, comfortable and waterproof.

When everyone else was wearing sandals or perhaps flip-flops, I wore these. I was quite fond of them. They covered up my feet and provided me with the comfort of shoes, while still being completely waterproof and weatherproof. They were great for boating, wearing around the beach, and basically any time others might wear sandals. I was too ashamed to wear anything that exposed my feet the way sandals did. My feet had looked bad for years. Even as a young man, I had ugly feet. My brother didn't. My mother didn't. My kids didn't. But, much like my father's, my feet had always been pale and unattractive. Thick, discolored nails adorned my feet like claws. Trimming, washing, and filing had failed to change their hideous appearance. Weathered and calloused from hard work and a lack of attention, my feet were a source of shame and embarrassment.

I used to think it was unfair. I never really complained about it. After all, who would I complain to? Even back when I graduated from college, my feet were ugly. That was over fifty years ago! Over time, I came to realized that I had been blessed with so many other things; the appearance of my feet seemed trivial in the big picture. It is much more important to have a healthy heart, bladder, kidneys, lungs, and pancreas. Of course, nobody sees any of them. I guess whatever beauty I might have possessed had always been on the inside. I had certainly been very healthy. I had once prided myself in going twenty years without having to see the doctor.

That was long ago, though. The days of never being sick had somehow passed me by just like technology had. My blood pressure was generally under control, and my cholesterol levels were better than those of most of my family. That little growth turned out to be a fatty tumor that posed no immediate threat. Still, I haven't gotten sick nearly as much as other people my age. But, come to think of it, there really aren't too many people my age left! My class reunions get smaller and smaller. Most people have died, while a few have moved off. There are still a few of us left, but not many.

Enjoying those wonderful shoes and their magnificent concealing properties, I carefully made my way across the sand. The soles were thin and flimsy. Their pliability made them give way to the uneven surface, making walking all the more difficult. With guarded steps, I slowly continued. I wanted to look up at the breathtaking panorama but felt obliged to look down to help my balance. When the way is unsteady, watching where you are going is critical. Just seeing the surface somehow helps your body connect to what it is doing—what to expect as each foot lands ahead.

I hesitated. I just wanted to see the ocean. Somehow my feet tried to keep going, even after my brain gave the signal to stop. I stumbled and fell forward into the warm, soft sand. I tried to get my hands out ahead of me to catch myself and break the fall, but they just would not go—at least not fast enough.

But it's funny how the mind works. What I thought as I fell was *I sure wish I had some hair to help break this fall!* As if a few strands of hair would have made any difference. I guess I had a few strands, but it was so thin and short I might as well have been bald.

When I hit the ground, I stuck in it. Having played a lot of sports, like football, I had always known how to hit and roll. That didn't work this time, not in the sand. I landed literally head first and stuck there. After a few seconds, I rolled over to one side. There was no sensation of pain. In fact, there was no sensation at all. I could not feel anything physical. I could see out, but I seemed trapped inside a body I could no longer control. As I lay there, I started to hear sounds, noises. People were yelling. I wondered what all the commotion was about, but I could not turn or stand to look around.

I noticed legs and then feet in front of me. *Why do everyone else's feet always look better than mine?* I pondered. There were adult feet and old feet there, but most of the feet looked young. Children with small, bare feet were everywhere. I wasn't sure where all the people had come from, but there seemed to be a lot showing up. I started to get up, but I just didn't feel like it. Not that I couldn't get up—I just didn't want to! That seemed good enough to excuse myself from trying. But somehow, in the back of my mind, I wasn't quite sure that I could get up, even if I tried. I was quite comfortable lying there. The sun was warm and, for the first time in a long time, there were no aches or pains. *Perhaps I should just relax a while and catch my breath.* After all that, I deserved a chance to catch my breath, didn't I?

Two

THE SUN SEEMED WARM AND gracious, just as inviting as ever. This may not have been exactly what I had in mind, but I was somehow still able to appreciate the beauty of this natural paradise that had been laid out before me. The constant wind still blew in off the ocean. The wonderful sounds filled my head along with the warmth and hospitality that seemed so native there.

I enjoyed the scenery, even from my awkward position. I continued to embrace it, losing myself in all that was. I felt so relaxed and peaceful. I felt I must truly be blessed to be so comfortable after such a fall. I could have easily hurt myself! But I was fortunate. There was no pain, no ache, nothing. The spectators were still buzzing around like bumblebees whose nest had been disturbed. Their feet were in constant motion around me. Their voices blended together like a buzzing melody. But their activities didn't seem very important right then. It's funny how falling seems like such a trivial thing when you're young.

In high school, I used to get slammed straight into the turf by a nose guard named Bubba three times a day and didn't think anything of it. And I also went down a few times while riding my motorcycle on a motocross track when I was in my twenties, and then on single-track trails through the woods into my thirties and forties. I remember one time when I wiped out spectacularly coming down a hill on what we used to call Loop 2.

I was on a brand-new KTM Enduro bike. It handled great and was incredibly fast. Why would I fall off a bike so stable? I was riding alone through some tight woods at a local mountaintop riding area. It was a private club, and all the members were fairly high-level riders, although some of them were getting older (and slower). The trails were what is called "single track," just barely wide enough for one bike to get through. When several guys rode together, they had to ride single-file, since the trail was far too narrow for two bikes to go beside each other. In some spots, the trail was so narrow the handlebars of one bike would not fit through. We used to cut the ends off our handlebars to make them narrower. Stock handlebars are around thirty-two to thirty-three inches wide. Mine were cut down to twenty-seven inches and still would not fit between the trees in certain spots. I would have to practically stop and wiggle my way through!

I came flying around a left hand corner at the top of a hill on Loop 2. As I came out of the corner, I headed back down the hill. It was not that steep, but the incline was sufficient to let you know you weren't on level ground. I had been telling myself how I was on the best woods bike made. Now I had no excuses for being slow. This was the latest state-of-the-art equipment that everyone else was salivating for—fresh off the showroom floor. It had just come out (early release of this model) and had been written up in a magazine as "the ultimate off-road weapon."

As I came out of the corner, I noticed a log across the trail. As everyone knows, logs never fall straight across a trail. It was at an angle, crossing the trail diagonally. As I shifted from second gear up into third, I brought the front wheel up into the air to cross the log. That went fine, but as my rear wheel hit the log, the speed and impact (maybe twenty plus miles per hour) kicked the back of the bike off to one side. The tree was wet, and the bark had been knocked off by an earlier rider, exposing a wet, slimy surface that was completely void of any traction whatsoever. As the log kicked the rear of the bike off to the right, I found myself heading straight for a tree. It was not a large tree, but it was large enough. As my front end came down, the bike bounced once. Before I could get settled and steady enough to react, *wham!* I had hit the tree. My head went to the left, and my right shoulder went straight through the tree—or at least it tried to!

When my body came to a stop, I was flat on my back on the ground in the middle of the trail. This huge pain echoed through my chest. It wasn't a dull pain; it was a sharp, penetrating pain. It felt like I had broken a rib and it was sticking out of my chest, right through a lung. Of course, this was not the case. But it is not an understatement of how it felt. I was in so much pain, I couldn't breathe.

I rolled over onto my knees, beside my motorcycle, which was still running. I reached over and hit the kill switch to turn the engine off. I then continued to attempt to breathe. I can't say I was gasping for air. I was not "gasping" at all. I wanted to but couldn't. It was as if a huge hand had covered my mouth, suffocating me. I was trying to inhale, but I could not get any air in past that huge hand obstructing my windpipe. I just didn't have enough strength, enough power, to bring air into my lungs. As I struggled and struggled, I remember thinking I was going to die. Not from the pain, not from the back or shoulder injury, but I would suffocate and die from lack of oxygen. It seemed like I struggled to breathe forever. I remember wondering how I had remained conscious. It may have only been for a few seconds, but that was certainly not my perception at the time.

Once I finally was able to breathe again, I tried to stand up. The pain in my back and shoulder had moved down into my chest and gut. Once my attention was no longer focused on breathing, the pain returned. I was alone, in the woods, in the middle of nowhere. I had to get out, no matter how much I hurt or how badly I felt. I could lie there for days or maybe weeks before someone else might come down that trail and find me.

I finally managed to climb to my feet. I stood there for a while, again focusing on breathing as the pain increased. I had to grit my teeth and bend over to get the bike. It didn't seem to be too badly damaged. Halfway leaning on the bike while it leaned on me, I managed to stand it up. I rested again a few moments before attempting to throw my leg across the seat. On the third try, I finally got my leg across the saddle. Now I was able to sit and quasi-relax while I continued trying to get my bearing.

"Okay," I said to myself. "This is a great bike, a new bike, and it always starts 'super easy.' Let's just hope it will again after being upside down." And, sure enough, it cranked right up on the first kick, as always. (Dirt bikes didn't have "sissy starters," a.k.a. electric starters, in those days.) I cut through the trees and got turned around. I headed backward down the trail, knowing that it was against all rules of decorum. It wasn't far back to a crossing over a fire road. I took it back to the main road and then back to camp. When I arrived, several others were sitting around "pit racing." (That's where everyone tries to see who can tell the tallest tale, but always with at least a grain of truth.)

I parked my bike and sat on the tailgate of my pickup truck. After removing my helmet and gloves, I fell back, almost collapsing into the bed of the truck. I lay there for probably twenty minutes. Eventually, one of the guys in the camp said, "Hey, are you all right?"

"Not sure," I said. "I fought with a tree and lost." After accepting some sympathies, I felt I should get loaded up and head home where I could get some real rest. They must have felt sorry for me, watching me try to load my bike, because they came and took over, loading it for me. I thanked them repeatedly and headed home.

That fall really hurt. Not just my ego, like falling in the soft sand, but it *really* hurt me. I had to go to home and then to work the next day and act as though I was all right. Standing straight and erect was truly a challenge! I seemed to lean to the left, unable to avoid favoring that side. Since my wife hardly approved of such folly as riding a motorcycle, especially in the woods, I felt compelled to hide my pain from my family as well as my coworkers. It must have been two months before I got a full night's sleep.

Of course, these days I barely ever get a full night's sleep anymore, even without any particular injury. There's always some little ache or pain to keep you awake when you're my age.

Some sand must have gotten into my mouth during the fall; I could feel the grit on my tongue. The feet were still gathered around, moving. I remembered how, in my football days, whenever someone was injured, the other players used to gather around in a group until a coach or someone showed up to wave everyone away. "Give him some room," they always used to say.

I still remember the coach saying that the first time I took a really big hit.

The grass on the field was freshly cut, but not short. It was tall and thick like carpet, providing a cushion upon which we could land. The loose cuttings were in neat rows awaiting our arrival. It was a cold day in October, but the sun was shining as we went to war. It seems ironic how seriously we took ourselves at that age. We stretched, warmed up, and prepared for the game. We went through all the same motions that a professional team would go through. We ran and jumped and hit each other, practicing our passing, catching, handing off, punting, and even kicking. We ran through offensive plays and defensive stunts. We yelled, barked, and growled with all the intensity of a mountain lion protecting her cubs.

I played tailback for the Wolverines, a fierce name for a team of nine-year-olds! At that time, I was reasonably fast and often ran sweep plays around the tight end. We were involved in a close game. Imagining ourselves to be great, with the fate of the championship at stake, we battled with all our hearts. The game was tied, and we had the ball. We had been moving the ball down the field but faced a fourth-down play. Only needing about a yard, we were going for the first down!

On this particular play, I was running the ball into the middle of the defense. Naturally, they were ready for me. I might not have been the biggest player on the team, but I was one of the strongest, hardest hitting players (or so I believed). I put my head down to run over somebody. After all, I had already determined that I would *not* be denied! How could I allow someone to stand in the way of my first down? When we hit, it was like two little bulls colliding (very small, young bulls that weighed about seventy pounds). I stayed down for an extra minute, wondering if I could get up at all. I could taste the dry dust in my mouth. With that beautiful green carpet to fall on, I somehow managed to find the only bare spot on the entire field. When I got up, I stood there a second and looked around. Everything looked as though it was colored differently. It was like a huge kaleidoscope of colors had been superimposed over the rest of the scenery. Things were red and blue and green and yellow.

The colors were all moving, but I wasn't. The images were not clear enough to focus my vision on any particular thing. Feeling rather shaky, I made it back to the huddle. I was trying to regain my composure, still somewhat amiss. Of course, I couldn't dare take myself out of the game, so I stayed in and tried to keep going. The coach may have sensed that I needed a break, because I didn't carry the ball for a couple of plays. I learned what it means to "shake the cobwebs out!" It was hard to imagine we could hit each other that hard, as little as we were. I think, looking back, I must have held my head and neck in just the wrong position at the moment of impact. But even shaken up, I didn't go out of the game. It took a play or two for me to regain my composure, but I managed to do so and kept going.

And that was pee wee football for kids in elementary school. I found out that bigger kids playing, let's say, college football, hit even harder! Instead of playing against guys that weighed seventy pounds, I found myself playing against guys that weighed 270 pounds. Some kids in elementary school are mean. However, they can hardly measure up to the disposition of an angry man in college who has accumulated more than twenty years of hostility, anger, and frustration. In every game and every practice, I faced that hostility. I was a running back and, for the defense, the running back might as well wear a huge target on his chest.

Of course, as a running back, you attempt to avoid those "on target" hits. But sometimes the situation dictates unavoidable collisions, such as the one that occurred during our intra-squad game at the culmination of our preseason training. The team was divided into two teams for the annual "Purple and White Game." When we divided our one team into two, there were only so many starters to go around. This meant all the starters and all the "second team" or backups would get to start or, at least, play a lot. They tried to play everyone so that the coaches could evaluate each player at each position to determine skills and usefulness in various potential situations.

I had been playing tailback on the purple team, and our offense had worked its way down the field and into scoring position. I had made a couple of good runs or pass receptions and felt pretty good about the way things were going. We were down at the goal line, trying to get the ball into the end zone for a touchdown. They gave me the ball on a running play up the middle (off the right guard). That's an honor, being given the ball at the goal line. The coaches must have wanted to see if I had what it takes to get the ball into the end zone (it was my rookie season, as a sophomore transfer).

The linebacker opposite me who would be trying to stop me just happened to be one of the stars of our defense. (The prior year, he had been voted all-American.) I was a typical running back for that era, about five feet eleven inches tall and weighing around two hundred pounds. The linebacker was about six feet three inches tall, and weighed around 240 pounds. Needless to say, he was quite a bit stronger than I was, too.

I lined up about six or seven yards deep in the backfield. I didn't think I should try to jump over the pile of players because the linebacker was so tall. I would have no leverage with my feet off the ground. I decided to hit the line low and hard. I was hoping for a gap—a seam I could exploit to break through for the couple of yards we needed. But when I hit the line, there was no seam. I collided with the linebacker head on—*mano a mano*. I had the greater, full-speed running start, but he was bigger and stronger. Usually when you collide head on, the person going faster and harder "delivers the lick," and the person standing still or going slower "takes the lick." You also tend to get a leverage advantage by being low. If you are ever standing straight up and get hit in such a manner, you *will* be punished.

I was so low at the point of contact I was almost on the ground! He somehow managed to bend his huge frame down to that same level, as low as he could possibly go. I had done everything right. I had done everything I could do. But when we hit, I swear the ground shook! I did not have room to make the impact at an angle, to create more of a glancing blow where I might be deflected off to the side and squeeze by for a yard or two. No, that wasn't possible. We hit squarely and at full speed. I was going to run over him, or he was going to run over me. We both attacked, powerful and fearless, with neither holding anything back. Something had to give in that collision—the weakest link. That weakest link turned out to be my shoulder.

He was fine, but I got up, in pain, holding my arm and shoulder. When I was attended to by the team physician, and he asked me to describe the pain, I told him it was burning. It felt like my shoulder was on fire. That being the symptom of a pinched nerve, he naturally assumed that prognosis.

He treated the pinched nerve by grabbing my hand and pulling up and down rapidly, causing my arm to move in a sort of waving motion. That forceful shaking of the arm is designed to dislodge the pinched nerve. The problem was that I had also dislocated my shoulder. While the treatment I had received was the correct, proper treatment for a pinched nerve, it was the worst possible response to a dislocated shoulder. I should have only been out a few weeks, but the treatment turned that into half the season.

I was so despondent that I lost that sense of pride and accomplishment I had felt by making the team, the college team. I didn't play the following year. I could have refused to let an injury keep me out of the game. Instead, I quit. I gave up. I walked away from the game I love. I always wondered, *what if?*

$\mathcal{T}hree$

I CLOSED MY EYES. I COULD still feel the sun on my face, but the sounds of voices and seagulls and lapping waves faded away. That didn't matter, though; they were merely distractions. It had been a while since I had taken some time for quiet reflection. Any awareness of the beach seemed like a distant memory. I was alone with my thoughts, transcending any awareness of time to which I had ever been accustomed.

I heard somewhere once that "to live life without regrets is to truly live." Perhaps that was true. I never wanted to have regrets; I never wanted to wonder, *what if?* Sometimes I lived without thought for the consequences, but at other times I had been far too timid and cautious. What if this was the end and I had lost all opportunity to conquer fear and to do those things I always wanted to do? I had always fancied myself destined for more and greater things, but I had always allowed fear and apprehension to stifle my courage.

There have been so many times when I made bad decisions

or simply wallowed around in doubt and confusion, not wanting to make any decision at all.

I did not want to depend on myself for the decisions and direction—I was looking for some divine assistance. I have quite often found in my life that direction never really came when I was looking for it. The guidance I have sought has often failed to manifest itself.

Sometimes, unexpectedly, I suddenly feel lost and abandoned. These thoughts haunt me when I remember the many times I needed someone to warn me, protect me, divert me, encourage me ... Seemingly "on my own," I made the worst possible decision, or so it seemed.

I remember playing baseball. I played Little League baseball when I was nine years old. I got to play on a very good team, the Tigers (we won the championship my last two years), but I generally didn't get to play the position I wanted to play. I had always wanted to be a pitcher. When I was eleven, I finally talked the coach into giving me a chance to pitch in a scrimmage game. My control was marginal, and my curve ball didn't usually break, but man, could I throw a fastball!

I pitched one inning. I faced four batters, walking one and striking out the other three. The closest anyone came to hitting the ball was a foul tip—just once! I gave up no runs, no hits, and struck out three batters, and never got to pitch again. The two coaches each had a son who pitched, and no one else ever did. It would have been easy to have been jealous and to have felt discriminated against, but they were probably the two best pitchers in the league. They were certainly and undoubtedly two *of* the best. When you win every game and the pitches strike out ten to twelve batters in a six-inning game, it's hard to fault them.

Our team was the league champion my last two years, when I was playing as an eleven- and then twelve-year-old. When I was eleven, we played hard in a very competitive league. We looked sharp and polished. In typical fashion, at least for me, I messed things up for myself.

Having won the league, we played in the local invitational tournament that featured the championship teams from all the nearby towns. When we played our first game in that tournament, we were pitted against the champions of the league in a town just a few miles away. This town was the rival of the town I played in. Their football and basketball teams (at the high school level) fought out this bitter rivalry every year. We beat them easily and made it to the finals, where we lost a close game and finished in second place in the tournament. Still, it had been a very successful season.

My mother, a school teacher, had coincidentally changed jobs and transferred to that same rival school district following my season playing as an eleven-year-old. I could continue to play for the same championship team I had been with for the past three years, or I could go through the draft process and play for a team in the new town in which my mother worked and I attended school. My parents told me that they would allow me to play in either town. When practice began for the team with which I had been playing, I started practice as always. People from the other town and from school had been trying to convince me to try out for Little League in the town I had begun attending school. They knew I had played on the really good championship team from the other city and thus assumed I must be pretty good myself.

I didn't know what to do. I liked my old team, but I was going to a new school now and needed to make new friends.

And, after all, I had always wanted to pitch. I knew I would never get a chance to pitch on my old team. Back in the other town where I had been playing, it was spring break, and there was no practice for two weeks. That made things easy. I decided to go ahead and at least tryout. Very few kids my age tried out, and the ones that did weren't very good. I was the first choice of the first round. In other words, the worst team in the league got the first selection, and they chose me. I went to practice for a couple of weeks (during my other team's break for the school system's spring break) and really had my eyes opened. I had not realized how skilled and professional my coaches had been. It definitely gave me a better appreciation for them. I was getting to pitch, but the team was horrible. Watching our practices, I could not imagine how we would ever win a game.

When the time came for my old team to start practicing again, I quit the new team and rejoined my old teammates as if nothing had ever happened. It seemed to be my little secret, and I thought them to be none the wiser. I started and played all year, as always. We went undefeated, not just winning the championship but decimating every team in the league. I think we averaged about an eight-run margin of victory for the season. After humiliating every team in the league, the announcements for the all-star selections were made. Every eligible player (to be eligible you had to be eleven or twelve years old) on our team was selected to be on the all-star team … except one person. Apparently, everyone had known about my little foray into the rival town's league. I was a traitor—disloyal—and did not deserve to represent our league on the all-star team. So players with lower batting averages, fewer stolen bases, and more errors took my place on the all-star team. I was denied that honor which would have meant so much to me at that time. I regretted my poor decision that somehow sabotaged my final year of Little League. I blamed myself at the time, though I looked back later and wondered if it had just been the hand of fate moving against me again.

Always a fighter, I would not succumb even to fate without a fight. I loved baseball and felt compelled to keep playing. I enjoyed the game and never seriously even considered giving it up. Stubborn and determined, I did finally get my chance to pitch when I got older.

After my Little League fiasco, I moved into the next league, as a thirteen-year-old, in the town in which I had been attending school. I went through tryouts and was drafted in the normal manner. There did not seem to be any repercussions from what had happened a year earlier. Once again, I was quickly drafted by the worst team in the league. One thing that really stood out to me was the general apathy and lack of commitment of the players on my team. I didn't understand it. I couldn't begin to explain it. It could have resulted from the coaching. We had fairly good coaches who were nice guys, but they were not as skilled and talented as my Little League coaches. I really hadn't understood how truly remarkable and amazing my coaches had been. Six or eight different guys about the same age in this little town went on to play college baseball. That's not so remarkable in itself, but that's just the number that played college baseball on teams that won national championships. Imagine that many people playing on one of three national championship baseball teams, all coming from that same humble start. Now that is truly amazing!

But now, in this higher league, the players skipped practice or loafed. They did not have the level of dedication or the level of skill necessary to win a championship. Maybe it was just the players, and not the coaches. Or perhaps as kids get older they get distracted by more things. Maybe going from a small field with two hundred-foot fences to a Major League size field (almost) with four hundred-foot fences was just too much for players to handle. Hitting was always the name of the game, and stretching the field so much made every park a pitcher's ballpark, rather than a hitter's ballpark. In Little League, players would often hit five to ten homeruns a season, even against good pitching. In the Babe Ruth League, with the bigger field, there might have been one homerun in the entire league during a period of four or five years. No one that age could knock it out of a park that big, at least not very often.

I remember going to one game where half the team had not showed up. I was there, as always, even though I was hurt. I had broken my arm during spring training for football. There were only eight other players that had come to the game. By rule, you must start the game with nine players. You may finish with less, generally due to injury, but you must start the game with nine. I had to start so that the team would not have to forfeit the game. I played centerfield. That was judged to be the position where my injury would least handicap our defense. The left and right fielders could cheat toward center to help cover for me.

It was my right arm that was broken. Being right handed, I caught the ball with my left hand and threw with my right hand. They hit a couple of balls to me in centerfield during the game. I caught the ball just fine—throwing it back in was the problem! The second baseman came running out to cut off my throw. I managed to make a decent throw and even got my picture in the local paper. They had a shot of me standing in the outfield with a cast on my right arm, suspended by a sling around my neck!

But as much as throwing the ball with the wrong arm was a challenge, batting with only one hand was really a challenge. The third baseman played in, looking for a bunt. The infield played way in, and the outfield was almost at the back edge of the infield dirt. Not accustomed to batting with only one hand, I wasn't sure which side to try to hit from. Being right handed, it seemed more natural to see the ball coming from that side of the plate. Therefore, I decided to try it from that side of the plate. Swinging with only my left hand, I would be backhanding it. Since no one really expected me to even make contact, I could relax without having to worry about failing to meet anyone's expectations, including my own. I had swung and missed once and then took a couple of bad pitches for balls. The pitcher had pressure building on him. He certainly wouldn't want to walk a one-handed batter! He threw a fairly easy pitch, just trying to get the ball over the plate. I hit an expectedly weak shot right over the pitcher's head. It landed around second base, but because the infielders had been playing me so far out of position, no one could get to the ball to make the catch! The next day at school, everyone teased and ridiculed the pitcher relentlessly! "Yeah, you're so bad he could hit your pitching with one hand." Or, "They say batters can hit your best pitches with one hand tied behind their back … or do they just leave it tied around their neck [in a sling]?"

But even my little victory was hollow. The outfielder had picked up the ball and thrown me out at first. I didn't actually get a base hit; I had just succeeded in making contact and not striking out. As always, even in my victory, I had been able to find defeat!

Playing in the Babe Ruth League for a lousy team had certain advantages: I got to pitch. My enthusiasm compensated for what I lacked in experience. Initially, I only pitched in relief after the starting pitcher allowed so many runs that winning seemed hopeless. But after only a couple of outings in relief, I finally got my chance to start. It was a day game on a Saturday afternoon. With the game beginning at four o'clock, I had all morning to mentally rehearse every pitch, imagining the batter and the situation. Time proceeded slowly as I contemplated the epic performance I was preparing to give. Hitting corners and embarrassing would-be batters is easy when you are imagining it flawlessly unfolding.

After a long morning of anxiously anticipating my chance to really pitch, not in relief, but as a starter, my chance was finally at hand. I warmed up as the team took infield, throwing a little harder than a more experienced pitcher would. The adrenaline was flowing! Dave, the catcher, had joked with me before the game. He kept trying to make me laugh, without success, to calm my nerves. He could tell I was excited and wanted to keep me focused for the start of the game. His jokes were not funny, and I was lost in my own thoughts, almost oblivious to what he said. He had no luck in diverting my attention, no matter how hard he tried. Then, as the game started, my first pitch was a low fastball right over the heart of the plate. He caught it in the palm of his catcher's mitt and moaned as it stung his hand. "Ste-e-e-r-r-i-k-e!" called out the umpire as Dave dropped his mitt and quickly started shaking his hand. Now, I broke out in laughter as did half the team. He couldn't make me laugh with his stupid jokes, but now, unintentionally, he got the reaction he could not solicit.

"Way to stop the ball," the third baseman said, snickering.

"Yeah, right," Dave sarcastically replied. But when Dave eventually looked up at me as he approached the mound after picking up the ball, he realized that I had been laughing, too. He broke into a smile, having been forced to laugh at himself, and said, "Okay, let's get this thing done."

"Yeah, I think it's time," I said. I still had butterflies, but now I felt like I could finally ignore them. He returned to the catcher's box as I mounted the rubber and awaited his signal: fastball outside to this left-handed leadoff hitter. I fired the next pitch quickly. The batter took a short hack at it and fouled the pitch back. With an 0-2 count, I was in command. My next pitch was high, well out of the strike zone for a ball. Knowing my control was only marginal, I aimed the next pitch at the middle of the plate. A curve ball that hung out there, barely breaking, the batter unloaded. He hit the ball around three hundred feet, right down the first-base line. Fortunately for me, it landed foul, harmlessly. I came back with a hard fastball over the outside of the plate. My heart fluttered as the batter swung and missed for strike three.

Caught up in the moment, it took a few seconds for the situation to register with me. The batter was running. I saw Dave scrambling to pick up the ball as the batter headed for first base. He hurriedly grabbed the ball and fired it at the first baseman. If our first baseman had been nine or ten feet tall, he might have been able to reach Dave's throw. But, being only six feet, he helplessly watched it sail over his head into deep right field. The right fielder, caught unaware, chased the ball down in time to hold the runner at third base.

I faced another batter and then another. I pitched with all my heart for the entire inning. After facing ten batters, I had given up five runs on one hit with one walk and five strikeouts, all in one inning. Batters consistently reached bases on errors, either by the catcher dropping the third strike or by a fielder dropping a batted ball. The other team had "batted around," even though I had given up only one single and one walk.

I came out for the second inning with similar results. I could not pitch well enough to compensate for the rest of the team's poor performance. Though I pitched only two and two thirds innings, I was the winning pitcher in my own mind. While my performance hadn't measured up to my imaginary, pregame heroics, I was satisfied with myself. I had pitched well enough that our opponents had not beaten us—we had beaten ourselves. With greater support from the rest of my team, I could have pitched a shutout or, at least, a respectable, winning performance. I felt good, somewhat vindicated, and went on to become a respected pitcher at that level. I had seemingly conquered Babe Ruth baseball.

As I got older, though, I moved up to Senior Babe Ruth for players ranging from sixteen to eighteen years old. And, yes, things were different then. The team I played on was really good. Almost every pitcher in the league was on my team. I'm not sure how it happened, but we probably had eleven of the best fourteen pitchers all on the same team. Everyone could pitch! That helped our batting, too. Since we had nearly all the good pitchers, our opponents always had weak pitching. We never had to face the really tough pitchers because they were on *our* team!

Not batting against the best pitchers helped a lot in Senior Babe Ruth. I thought I was a pretty good hitter through Little League and Babe Ruth, but when I started playing high school baseball, it became painfully obvious that my hitting was substandard. The high school team is like an all-star team for the whole city. The best fifteen to twenty guys between the ages of fifteen and eighteen all play for the same high school team … in every town. Our team may have been our town's best, but every team we played was comprised of the best players of that respective city's league. When I was merely fifteen, I found myself trying to bat against a player who would have a scholarship to pitch in Division One baseball for an ACC, SEC, or Big Ten conference school. I found that to be a very humbling experience.

Maybe I wasn't as good as I thought I was. I had played with people who were good enough to compete on that level; I just wasn't one of them. I figured a baseball career for me just wasn't meant to be. Destiny would have her way with me, but not until I had a few more hoorays! My hitting was still mediocre, but I tried to convince myself that pitchers didn't have to be good hitters. I seemed to perform fine as a pitcher at the city league level, but pitching in high school was a different matter. The older players were at a whole different level. They had been playing for years. Generally, only the players who are the most serious, most dedicated, and most skilled continue to play through the age of eighteen. It seems like most guys in high school lose interest by this time.

By the time I got to high school, my repertoire had grown substantially. I could throw a fast ball, a curve, a changeup, and a submarine that tailed away from left-handed hitters. My control had improved, but there were higher standards as well. This meant my control was still just marginal, even though it had improved. I remember one game I pitched in high school. It was fairly late in the game, and we were behind. I threw a good fastball right down the inside of the plate to a right-handed hitter. He killed it! The guys on the other team told us it was the first homerun that batter had ever hit. It went out of the park in centerfield, where the fence is deepest. The fence was probably 440 feet. That's a long way for a sixteen-year-old kid to hit a baseball!

It made me realize that maybe I wasn't such a good pitcher after all. This guy wasn't a great batter and had never once hit a homerun. The one time he connected *would* be against me. I could rationalize, "Yeah. If you always swing for the fence, sooner or later you're bound to get lucky." It seemed like I still just couldn't get a break. Was it fate or just coincidence? Maybe if I had trained harder or practiced more …

Four

THE BLAZING SUN ON THE hot beach sand should have burned my tender, old skin, but somehow it didn't. Heat, that's what I felt instead—heat. The warm, delicious radiance of the sun seemed to blanket my body. The warmth of the sun felt calming, but within I felt a horrible pain. It was not the feeling of fear or even physical pain—it was the feeling of remorse, of failure. How much the fear of failure drives us! I wonder if it scares everyone as much as it scares me.

We all make mistakes and pay for them. Perhaps I have just been in the wrong place at the wrong time. Maybe fate has predestined me to suffer. Or, maybe I had everything going for me, but I made a stupid decision. Ah! There's the rub!

Stupid decisions! I read an entire novel while driving home from Florida. I drove eight hundred miles with a book propped on the steering wheel of my car! As stupid as that might have been, I actually made it without accident or calamity. I guess the subconscious mind takes over for the conscious mind when it becomes unable or unwilling to think for itself. Or, perhaps it was just a higher power looking out for me?

But then there were accidents where I had not been the one who was stupid! The worst wreck I have ever been involved was like that. Back in the early 1990s, I was sitting at a traffic light in my small, two-door sports car when a lady approaching the intersection lost control of her car. She was coming down a hill on a wet road and could not stop. She evidently swerved because her BMW 735 (a much larger, heavier car than mine) was spinning around in the road. She came across three empty lanes to collide head-on with my motionless car. Her car was moving downhill with all the speed and momentum.

My car was crushed. I probably should have been killed, at least according to the laws of nature and physics. It seems that having designed and authored those laws, God did not see fit to place himself subject to them. They cut me out of the car and rushed me to Vanderbilt Hospital (it was not the closest hospital, but due to the nature and severity of my wounds, the medics felt that it would be necessary to take me to the best facility around if I was to have any chance of survival). I spent several days in the Intensive Care Unit. I was hospitalized for a week. I underwent several reconstructive surgeries to put me back together.

It was a difficult and trying ordeal for me, and even more so for my family. My wife took off work to stay with me at the hospital while I was in critical condition. My parents came and stayed with me. One day my wife brought my young son, who was less than two years old. He knew that Daddy was gone and hadn't come back. Momma was gone all the time, even late at night, but at least she kept coming back home. My mother had been staying with him while my pregnant wife stayed with me at the hospital. When he saw me at the hospital, he was terrified and overjoyed at the same time. He was so happy to see me, but troubled by my appearance. My face was badly cut. One ear was almost ripped off. It was torn into three pieces and required a skin graft from my hip to reconstruct.

His joy was much more complete when I was finally able to return home. For days, he went around saying in the sweetest, most loving and innocent voice, "Daddy's home! Momma's home! My daddy's home!" His love was so pure and sincere, the same way our love needs to always be. It was not selfish or conditional. He did not seek personal gain or possess any ulterior motive. He felt the pure, simply joy of honest love.

I probably never appreciated or thanked my family enough for what they endured afterward. I was in tremendous, constant pain. My prognosis was quite bleak, at best. I was told I would never walk again, at least not normally. I would be able to get around, but only by enduring severe pain and discomfort. I would never be able to play sports again. The doctor suggested that I could perhaps play golf or go bowling, although even they might be too physically demanding for my limited strength and mobility.

The bones in one ankle had been completely crushed. They were described as being "like powder that had to be scraped out." I was blessed to have an orthopedic surgeon who was as much a gifted genius in the operating room as he was an arrogant jerk outside the operating room. A T-shaped metal plate with about fourteen metal screws had been inserted into my right leg. My ankle had severely limited mobility and was filled with a dull, constant throbbing. With every heartbeat, I could feel the blood coursing through my veins as my ankle remained swollen to more than twice its normal size. My left ankle had been previously damaged in an accident ten years earlier. The ligaments had been torn and had never had the full rest needed to properly heel. Now they were torn again. The surgeon reported seeing visual evidence of scar tissue from the prior damage. That ankle typically bothered me more than the one that had been crushed.

My reconstructed ankle was so badly damaged that the orthopedic surgeon mentioned a procedure to help me deal with the pain. He said he could perform another surgery where he would fuse the bones in my ankle together, effectively eliminating it as a working joint. He never recommended such a drastic step unless the pain was so unbearable that it was necessary just to function. If that surgery was performed, I would lose 100 percent of the mobility in that ankle, but it wouldn't hurt anymore.

I wanted to avoid such an extreme measure if there was any way possible. I had a permanent partial disability rating due to the loss of use of that leg, and to a lesser extent, the other leg. The joint was already becoming beset with arthritis. The arthritis would continue to worsen and cause more and more pain, stiffness, and problems. For the rest of my life, I would have no chance at all of ever recovering significantly. I could never play softball or tennis. There was no hope of ever being able to play basketball or volleyball, not even a pickup game. I had become a helpless, hopeless cripple with no chance for any real recovery.

I tried physical therapy. That could increase my range of motion some, but probably not appreciably. I worked hard at the physical therapy, but to no avail. It made little difference in my physical condition, just as the doctor had predicted. But to whom do desperate men turn when all hope seems lost? Yes,

God. I threw myself at His feet, asking for His mercy. As is His nature, He was generous with abundant mercy and forgiveness. It seems that He was unaware that I had been given no hope of recovery.

It took years of dedicated work, but I reached a complete recovery. The dedication was much more spiritual than physical. As my children grew up and played sports, neither of them could outrun me before the age of thirteen or fourteen, even though I was reaching well into my forties by then. I taught and coached basketball. I played one-on-one with a college basketball player on scholarship and was more than competitive. I coached tennis and competed against professionals, players on college scholarships, and even nationally ranked players, and I either beat them or at least played them competitively. Not bad for someone with no chance of recovery!

But the credit is not mine to take. The only thing I can take credit for is going to the Lord. Beyond faith, belief, and prayer, I did little to perpetuate my recovery. The credit and the glory, as always, is God's. I am afraid to try to steal God's credit for this miracle. I realized that what God had done had made a huge impact on my life, but what had I done to make an impact on other people's lives, a *positive* impact?

$\mathcal{F}ive$

DURING MY LIFE, I SUPPOSE I have made a few feeble attempts to help another person, but those would hardly qualify as capable of changing the direction of someone's life. Those attempts were weak and not very valiant. Even when we have been given so much, it is easy to live our own lives, unaware of the pain and misfortune around us, caught up in our own day-to-day concerns without extending help to those around us in need. It is so easy to overlook the many gifts that you are blessed with. Everyone does that, don't they?

It seems so easy and natural to dwell on all the things that are lacking, even to the exclusion of recognizing the things that are abundant. If you already have something, there is no need to worry about that. Instead, you worry about the things you don't have. Perhaps that is greed, envy, or maybe just a good capitalist drive to get ahead. Like Waylon Jennings said in his song, "… we've been so busy keeping up with the Jones's, a four car garage and we're still building on. Baby, it's time we got back to the basics of love."

Everyone wants to be comfortable, but when we seek too much comfort, too much gratification, and too many "things," we become narcissistic and materialistic, leaving behind the delicate balance between adequate and comfortable. Sometimes the opportunity to help others is not sought out but is instead thrust upon us by God, chance, or perhaps the forces of nature. I spent one summer in Albuquerque, New Mexico, and found myself confronted by such an opportunity.

At the tender age of nineteen, I was wearing a Fellowship of Christian Athletes shirt from high school while dining in a Denny's restaurant. I had finished eating and was approached by a fairly young, unkempt girl. Without makeup, her long, stringy, dark hair conveyed that she was probably not even eighteen years old yet. She stammered, uncomfortably, "Umm … ugh … excuse me, mister." (I thought that was especially strange since we were almost the same age.) "I noticed your shirt."

"Yes?" I answered.

"Are you one of *those*? A Christian?" she asked. "I saw your shirt …"

"Well, yes, as a matter of fact, I am," I replied. I could not imagine what was coming next! Perhaps it would be some insightful question about my philosophy or about my religious ideas. She did not look like the type to pose such questions, but who knows what lies underneath the rough exterior of someone who has been long challenged by life?

"Can I ask you something?" she quietly asked. She spoke, not from intellectual curiosity, not from a desire to learn, not even from confusion, but from a painful place filled with fear and anxiety. Her voice was filled with a quiet desperation, as if this was her last hope, her last chance, to salvage her life. What forces could threaten and intimidate her so? Surely I could not refuse!

"Sure," I answered. "What do you want to know?" I secretly wondered if *I* really wanted to know!

She hesitated, as if she could not find the right words. "Is God real? Is Jesus real?" She paused, and then continued, "And how do you know they are real?" Clearly, her focus was on that which she was lacking.

"Well, you said you saw my shirt ... At FCA camp—that is, Fellowship of Christian Athletes camp—I was with a group of guys up on top of a mountain in North Carolina. We ate together and played sports or games and just got to know each other. We were all becoming friends. We talked and shared stories and just had fun. But every evening, it seemed like the hot summer winds would blow in rain clouds and we'd have a storm—only for a little while, maybe, but it would rain almost every afternoon."

"I used to hate the rain," she said. "It always seemed so dreary. But now it's different. I welcome the rain when it comes. Sometimes, I even go out and stand in it. But even the hardest rain can't wash away ..." She paused and then stammered a little. "I'm sorry. What were you saying about the camp?"

"Well, on one particular afternoon, it rained really hard," I continued. "It poured and poured for almost an hour. There was thunder and lightning! It was so loud and so close that the camp counselors assembled everybody together in one area. When they did, there was one guy missing!"

"Oh!" she exclaimed. "What happened?"

"They went back to his room to look for him, but he wasn't

there. They checked the cafeteria and the bathrooms, but he wasn't there, either. They looked everywhere, but no one could find him. We could tell that the staff looked worried and upset. They must not have been used to anyone being missing! Finally someone came running up to the head counselor and said that he had gone out hiking on a trail across the mountain about thirty minutes before the storm hit. At this point, it was still raining heavily, but something had to be done. They assembled a crew of counselors to go out after him."

"Did they ever find him?" she asked.

"Yes. They followed the trail he had left on. About an hour later, they showed back up at camp with the missing hiker. He had been out on the trail hiking and had been struck by lightning! He had been wearing a rather large silver-looking cross. We didn't know if the metal had attracted the lightning, almost killing him, or if it had absorbed or reflected the impact and saved his life."

"I can't even imagine getting struck by lightning," she confessed.

"I *can* tell you this," I said, pausing several moments, "with great certainty, *being struck by lightning is a traumatic, coming-to-Jesus type of experience!* It was definitely life-changing for him, and it also made a big impact on everyone around who had witnessed his experience or, at least, the aftermath of it."

As I looked at the girl, I could see in her face the effect of my words. She had gotten caught up in the story. I don't tell stories that well, but the truthfulness and sincerity in my voice demonstrated my attitude toward those events. "I can't explain it. I know it doesn't sound reasonable. Believe me, I'm not prone to making up tales such as this ... but, I swear I could feel the presence of God on that mountain!" I proclaimed with a crescendo. Realizing I might have become too loud, I looked around apologetically at the faces in the restaurant. "Sorry," I said.

"It was kind of like going into a football stadium for a big game, and you can feel the electricity in the air. I don't know if you've ever done that, but a blind, deaf person who did not know where he was could tell the difference. You really can feel it! It was like that on the mountain—you really could feel it! I know God is real because I have felt Him, I have experienced Him, and I have done so in a very solid, objective sort of way—not just lying in bed and imagining God in a vivid way that seems real! Why do you ask such a question?"

"Well," she answered, "let me tell you a story. My brother and I ... well, I guess we've done some bad things. He would drink and smoke pot, and when he'd get high, he would want to go do things."

"What kind of things?" I asked.

"Well," she hesitated, clearly reluctant to explain. "They would sit around in a circle and burn incense. They would smoke pot, too, while they were doing it. They drew emblems and lit candles. They chanted, and sometimes they would sing these weird songs. Sometimes, they would even get up and take their clothes off and dance naked! Well, really, they were worshipping the devil!" She faced me with a most unusual look, one of shame, guilt, regret—and yet one of innocence.

"I did not do *that!* I never agreed with what they were doing! But he was bigger than me, and sometimes he would make me come along. He made me do things I didn't want to do!" she cried out, beginning to sob.

I did not know what to say. I had never encountered such an individual or experienced such things as these. I was curious, but at the same time I was scared myself! I had no idea what to say to her or how to respond. I tried to comfort her, because I did not know anything else to do. "Hey! It's okay. Listen, it's all right now," I managed to spit out. "You're away from there now."

"Yeah," she said, "but I've got to go back. He's my brother. I live with him. I'll see him tonight when I get home. You don't understand how he is!"

"He won't try to hurt you, will he?" I asked.

"I don't know what he might try to do to me after tonight," she responded. She did not seem to have been telling me everything.

"Why? What happened tonight?" I inquired. "Why is tonight any different from any other night?"

"Tonight they had a ceremony. It was some kind of initiation or something. I didn't want to go! I didn't want to—I promise!" She had nothing to justify to me, yet she argued for herself as if I were sitting on the almighty seat of judgment.

"They had the ceremony at the room—the one where they always meet. Then we left to go home. We go right by a cemetery on the way home. A lot of times, I'll cut through there because it's shorter. My brother and his friends that were there told me not to."

I nodded in agreement, acknowledging her words.

"There's a place where the fence is pulled down lower. You can get over it there pretty easy. It's maybe only three or four feet high. I like to go that way because my dad is buried there. I know it's kinda creepy going to a graveyard, but I like to visit my dad there."

I was truly sympathetic. I had lost my father, too. I still go to the cemetery where my father is to visit him.

"I talk to him, and sometimes I feel like he might even be listening. But every time my brother tried to get across it, something kept knocking him back. He pulled it down and stepped across two or three times. Every time he did, there was something that kept knocking him back. He had to go around it to get home. When I saw him, his fingertips were bleeding, kinda bad, too! He told me, 'You weren't supposed to go in there!'"

"Why not?" I couldn't help but wonder aloud.

"I don't know. He just said I wasn't supposed to," she answered. "But he was mad! Really mad! I don't think I've ever seen him so mad!"

"What's going to happen now?" I asked.

"I don't know, and I'm really afraid to find out," she confided. "What do you think I should do?"

I couldn't tell her what I was thinking. I would have told her to go find a priest or an exorcist or somebody, anybody but me! I could not tell her that. She had come to me and confided in me, seeking help. I could not turn away, no matter how much I wanted to do so, without offering some kind of help or advice. "Can you go home? Will you be safe there?" I asked.

"Well, I will be if my mom is home," she said. "But she's at work now. She won't be home for another hour. Can I stay with you until then?"

I was so relieved. I was afraid she would ask me to face her brother or to confront him and all his evil friends with her. The last thing I wanted was a bunch of drunken, satanic, pot smoking, devil worshipping heathens out to get *me*! "Sure," I told her. "We can wait here."

We sat down at a table and killed another hour and a

half before she left. She assured me that she would be fine. Somehow, I knew she was right.

Although I did not do that much for her, perhaps it had been enough. She probably needed someone to talk to and someone who could reassure her more than anything else. I may not have done much, but I had done that. And when she told me that she was going to be all right, I already knew it was true. I could tell that someone, something, was watching out for her. It was as if her life had some great purpose that had yet to be fulfilled. God was not going to allow anyone to derail her from the fulfillment of that purpose.

Sometimes I have not recognized for what purpose I should be striving, yet I have felt the hand of God protecting me, much like He was protecting that girl from her brother and his friends. Whether it is saving me from others or even saving me from myself, I have felt the protection and safety of God's hand upon my life.

Yes, God's hand upon my life, I wondered again—so strongly, so vividly, I was not sure if I had uttered those words aloud. I could again feel the sun's warmth upon my skin. I had a distant, vague awareness of the beach. *Are there people here?* I wondered. *Or just feet?* Overcome by my thoughts, I lost myself again in contemplation and introspection.

It was as if my awareness was pulled away from the beach by some outside force, yet I was strangely aware of the force at work. I contemplated how and why. It seems that sometimes, out of the blue, I suddenly get a thought or urge to do or say or read something that has been far from my mind, at least my conscious mind of which I am aware. Is this a message from God or some connection with a greater universal consciousness? I suppose these thoughts must be sent to warn me, protect me, divert me, or encourage me. It seems that sometimes, against all odds, a highly unlikely event will defy probability and miraculously occur to save me! Does my life have some great purpose I have yet to fulfill? What great thing have I ever done or will I ever do? It seems that all I have really done is work.

At one time, I was working delivering medicine and pharmaceuticals to hospitals, nursing homes, pharmacies, etc. My day began early, around 5:00 a.m. Some medicines have to be kept in a temperature-controlled environment, so I had gotten into the habit of always carrying two coolers with me. One cooler had ice packs to keep refrigerated items cool, while the other cooler contained dry ice to keep things frozen. I rarely needed the dry ice, but I was in the habit of always carrying it anyway.

One particular morning, it was raining. It wasn't pouring, but it was more than enough to get you soaked. I was wearing a raincoat to stay dry. The coat had been a Christmas present, one of those heavy raincoats made out of a rubberized material. It fit loosely, so it could be worn over normal clothing. It was extraordinarily water repellant, but it was also very hot.

One of my vices is to drink Diet Coke almost constantly. Every day I would carry a huge 44-ounce cup full and a full two-liter bottle with which to refill it. That saved me time and money. I didn't have to take the time to stop, park, go into a store, wait in line, come back out to the van, and get back into traffic. Certainly, a two-liter bottle was cheaper than just one extra-large drink from a store. And, it was big enough to refill my cup more than once! This particular day, my two-liter bottle was not very cold, and I didn't have any ice. I needed some way to cool my bottle of Diet Coke off fast, so I put it into the dry ice. Realizing that the greater the surface area exposed to the cold temperature (of the dry ice), the more quickly the liquid would be cooled, I did not just place the bottle into the dry ice, but I turned it upside down first! If I may offer a word of advice, *don't try this at home!* When I opened the screw-off cap on the bottle, I paid no attention to the "full" new feeling of the bottle. There was a piece of ice frozen in the very top of the bottle, immediately under the cap that I had unscrewed. Great! Now I couldn't get anything to drink out! I left the cap off so the warm air could get to the little chunk of ice and help it to melt.

I then proceeded into my next stop and delivered the medicine they needed. After I finished that delivery, I got into my van and prepared to leave. I had been wearing my raincoat all day, though it had not been raining for several hours. As I was about to leave, I realized that I needed to call my wife. Such a phone call is hardly ever brief, so I felt it necessary to plan to be on the phone for several minutes.

Directly across from me was an empty gravel lot that would be perfect for making such a call. I could sit there, undisturbed, for as long as I needed. It would be quiet, private, perfect. As I started into the lot, I noticed there was no traffic coming down either street. Although I had already pulled out of my parking space, preceded down the drive, and arrived at the empty street, I stopped.

I felt strangely compelled to take my raincoat off, right then and there. The logical thing to do would be to hurry across the street while it was clear. My plan was to stop there anyway. That was where I should remove my raincoat. Who would stop a moving car, less than thirty seconds away from their destination, just to do something that could easily wait? I had been needlessly wearing it for several hours since the rain had stopped. What difference could another few seconds possible make?

Still, I felt a sudden urge, a compulsion, to stop and take my raincoat off. So, I did. As I mentioned, the raincoat fit loosely. It took several seconds to come to a complete stop, shift the transmission into park, and open the door. Once I had done that, the time during which I was out of the vehicle to actually remove the coat was probably not more than two or three seconds. As soon as I stepped out of the van, *pow!* I heard a huge explosion that sounded like a gunshot! A piece of ice about the size of a small cork had been fired out of the two-liter bottle. The way I had placed the bottle right side up, on the floor, between the seats, it was pointed (or should I say aimed) directly at my temple. Had I not gotten out of the van at that precise moment, it would have been propelled into the side of my head, striking me in the eye, the temple, or perhaps another delicate area around my face. Getting out could have very well saved my life, and at the very least, prevented hospitalization.

The length of time I was at a safe distance removing my coat was only for a few seconds. That necessitates a precise window of avoidance. The margin for error, while still retaining the element of safety, was no more than plus or minus seconds, and probably not that much. I tried to calculate the odds of wearing the raincoat needlessly, and then removing it at precisely the right moment to avoid injury. As well as I could determine, the probability was many million to one against that ever randomly occurring. The odds of buying one lottery ticket in my life and winning it all with that one chance are better than the odds of randomly stopping that way to remove my coat.

You can wonder whatever possessed me to suddenly stop, but I know what possessed me. I don't have to wonder; it was an act of God. I don't know if my life was being spared or if I was just saved from a great deal of pain, expense, and inconvenience. That detail is not what is most important, though. The fact that the Lord came to my rescue is the prevailing theme I take away from that incident. Sometimes I think the biggest job the Lord has to do (relative to watching over me) is just to protect me from myself!

Six

LORD KNOWS I'VE DONE SOME stupid things. There was the time I tried to break the world's record for the longest jump on a bicycle. Now how smart was that?

The little rural town where I grew up had no red lights and very few stop signs. At least we had paved roads. Nearly all the buildings were old, even the houses, which were inevitably white frame houses. The bricks in the few downtown businesses looked old: the corners were rounded and weathered with pits and cracks covering most of the red bricks. It did have a railroad track, like nearly all small, rural southern towns. The intersection where the road crossed the railroad track was a three-way stop. On one side of the tracks, all three roads came together with stop signs on each one. The fourth road crossed the railroad tracks and *then* joined the other roads. There was no stop sign crossing the railroad tracks. The road opposite that one (the one that went directly across the tracks) not only had a stop sign, but also a hill.

The hill was plenty long and steep. My buddy Tom sat at the intersection on his bicycle to watch for traffic. Tom was slender but muscular. He never seemed to have many interests, but all his interests interested me, and he was fantastic at each of the few things he pursued. I came flying down the hill as fast as I could go, probably around thirty-five to forty miles per hour. After crossing the tracks, I had to turn left. The turn was not very sharp, but at the speed I would be going it would be impossible to pedal the bike around the turn. If I tried to pedal with the bicycle leaned over as far as would be required, the pedal would hit the ground. As hard and fast as I would have to be pedaling, I might wreck from just trying to pedal around the corner!

We had built a ramp in the dirt and gravel just off the road. It would launch me off into a grassy area that was relatively smooth. My hope was that, in the event of a mishap, the grass would provide a softer landing than the gravel or asphalt. (See, I was being extra safety conscious!)

I made the corner and managed to pedal a few more times before hitting the ramp. I bounced the bike just before impact and tried to pull it up into the air as far as possible. I was not quite skilled enough to accomplish this maneuver perfectly. When the bike became airborne, the back end went out to one side, probably from the momentum of making the corner. I don't know what the landing looked like, but it must have surely been a sight to behold! I flipped over several times, but still got up and walked away basically unscathed. Of course, no one wore helmets back then.

The jump was huge! We had a measuring tape that we used to measure from the lift off point to the point where I touched down. I am not really sure now, but it seemed like I jumped 126 feet. It should have barely broken the listed world's record, or at least have been within a foot or two. But the jump didn't count because I didn't land it! Crashing over a jump is not considered for world-record status.

That was probably just as safe as the time we raced a motorcycle against a sled. One winter, there was a snowstorm and school was closed. The other side of that same big hill was steeper, with one turn about one third the way down. Tom and I had been out playing in the snow all day. We were able to go pretty fast on the sled—*but just how fast?* we wondered. It is awfully hard to judge the speed of a sled you are riding when you are maybe four to six inches off the ground.

We thought that riding the motorcycle beside the sled would provide a better basis of comparison. The other side of the hill was long enough and iced over well enough to ride the sled all the way down. The shadow cast by the trees had kept one side of the road completely frozen—a solid sheet of ice. The other side of the road was wet, with ice in spots where it had not completely melted. My buddy and I took turns racing each other. We would start the motorcycle and leave it leaned over on its side stand, idling. One person would lie face down on the sled with his knees bent and his feet up in the air. The other person would push him while grasping his feet, using them like the handle on a shopping cart being raced across the grocery store. One person would push the sled and rider as fast as possible down the hill. He would stop pushing about ten to fifteen feet before they reached the motorcycle (a Honda XR70). This would allow time to regain balance and get to the motorcycle as quickly as possible to chase the sled.

While the sled seemed incredibly stable at any speed, the motorcycle did not. On the sled, we were a few inches off the ground. That ultra-low center of gravity seemed to provide the feeling of stability. The sensation of riding a motorcycle, even a small one, down a steep incline was not reassuring. The tires slipped and skidded unpredictably. We were so uncomfortable riding it in this manner that we would keep our feet off the foot pegs, sliding them along on the ground to catch us if we started to fall. Once or twice when we did fall, it didn't help. Our extended leg had no way of gaining enough traction to provide support.

We knew the little Honda had a top speed of around sixty miles per hour, so that would make it much easier to judge the actual speed the sled was traveling. We took turns; one time he would ride the sled and I would push, and the next time we would switch. The motorcycle was consistently able to overtake the sled by the bottom of the hill, but it was always a close race. The sled just barely lost. We estimated that the top speed of the sled was close to fifty miles per hour. The funny thing was that we never felt like we were going all that fast on the sled! And even in the slick conditions, we never wrecked or had even a slight mishap on that ice. Now *that* was a miracle!

The snow and ice of winter sports seemed to bring out the ridiculous daring in me! The first time I ever went skiing, I was a freshman in college. It was a trip sponsored by the student government at school. The school had arranged for a bus to go to the mountains to a ski lodge. The lodge was atop the mountain with an ice-skating rink and typical resort accompaniments.

Well, the legal drinking age at that time was only eighteen. College students are pretty much all eighteen or older. In order to help us relax and to make the bus ride more enjoyable, refreshments had been provided. Some of these happened to be alcoholic, and being typical all-American college students, we didn't want to risk offending the people who had so graciously arranged all this for us. We felt obligated, duty bound as it were, to partake in the refreshments, which of course included beer.

Surprisingly enough, we had become somewhat inebriated by the time we arrived at the ski resort. No one was commode-hugging drunk, but most of us felt pretty good. I departed from the bus, anxious to give skiing a try. Even though I had never skied before, I always thought it looked easy. As we arrived at the top, they checked us through a line and asked what size skis we needed. I thought the little short ones didn't look very manly. After all, I had played sports and weighed a good 170 pounds. I was bound to need longer skis to support all that weight!

I think I asked for two-forties or two-sixties, not even entirely sure what that meant. I had just noticed while I waited in line that bigger skis had bigger numbers associated with them. I made my way to the slopes and got my skis strapped on tightly. The advanced slope was closed for night-time skiing. There was one intermediate slope open and a beginner slope.

The beginner slope was so flat it hardly sloped at all. After trying the beginner's slope, which only had you moving at a snail's pace, I felt like advancing to the intermediate slope. Being dark and cold and winter, the temperature outside was around fifteen degrees. I had no idea the slope was icy and frozen. I took the ski lift up to the top of the intermediate slope. When it was my turn, I went over to the edge and looked down. The slope looked like it went straight down! After studying it for a few moments, I gathered up my courage and carefully pushed the front of my skis over the edge.

As I started down, I tried to go side to side like they do on television. The hill was so steep and slick that I could barely steer at all. I was essentially skiing on a sheet of ice, with little or no loose snow on top. Unable to curb my speed in that manner, I chose to go straight down. Not feeling very stable, I bent over into a tuck position. I immediately noticed that such a stance was much more stable. What I did not notice was how much faster I started going. It seems the ski racers use that posture for reasons other than just stability.

I was moving at a surprising speed. With my long skis and tucked posture, I was really able to get going. Moving with a full head of steam, I noticed that the fence at the base of the mountain where the ski ramp loaded was getting closer and closer. *No problem*, I thought. I straightened up and angled the nose of my two skis together. That forms a breaking maneuver called the "snow plow." The trouble was, there was no snow to plow through. Instead, I was skating across a sheet of ice. When I started getting really close, and still had not slowed down any to speak of, I had a brain storm … *I'll just turn my skis sideways like they do in the Olympics and stop that way!* Or so I thought.

My skis immediately went flying out from under me, and I landed flat on my back. As I was sliding along, I could see the other skiers on the ski lift looking over the edge at me, laughing and pointing. It was okay, though. Being ever so quick on my feet (or in this case on my back), I brilliantly used the wall to slow me down. It worked great. In fact, I stopped almost instantly. Somewhere through that ordeal, I broke my ski pole. I took it back and got it replaced.

Only a little discouraged, I decided to go back and try it again. After all, only my pride had really been injured. Come to think of it, maybe I was more intoxicated than I realized …

The next trip was quite different. Without any experience, mogul skiing was more difficult than it appeared to be on television. Once I got going in a particular direction, changing direction became a monumental task. I was trying so hard not to repeat my earlier mistake that I steered off in the other direction. I saw a roped-off section in front of me apparently being used for a class. I was headed straight for them despite my best efforts to turn left and head back around the corner and down the mountain. As they watched my approach, they clearly became more distraught than me. There were students panicking and trying to get out of the way as I got closer and closer. It must have looked like a scene from *Dumb and Dumber* as I headed in their direction. The instructor and the students were falling everywhere trying to get out of my way as I came through the roped-off area unable to stop! I still managed to have a good time, not get hurt, and drink even more social beverages on the return trip back to campus! Looking back, surely someone was looking out for me. But had I been looking out for anyone?

$\mathcal{S}$even

THOSE WINTER SPORTS WERE A far cry from the beach I found myself on. Surrounded by the sunshine and strangers, I was sitting upright. *What happened? I remember coming to the beach, but how did I get down here?*

As the questioned blazed through my head, I vaguely remembered falling. *But how did I get to be sitting here, upright? Someone must have lifted me,* I concluded. The people around seemed a little frantic, but I couldn't figure out why. I started to say something, but I didn't have anything to say. I didn't know what to say. I just sat there.

Then it hit me—*this will probably ruin my trip!* I wasn't hurting anywhere. There was no pain, but I didn't think I could get up. I really didn't want to get up. I was content just to sit there ... and rest. I needed a break. I had put a lot of miles behind me, and now I was just plain tired. Heck, I *deserved* a break.

I sure wish these people would calm down, though. It is so hard for me to relax with all this commotion. Why can't people just go on about their own business and leave me alone? Not that they were doing anything in particular *to* me. It's just that with so many people hovering around, how could I possibly relax or be the least bit comfortable? The little girl with sandals had bows on each shoe—just like Christmas. The guy in the red shirt kept putting his fingers up in my face. What did he expect me to do, anyway? I figured the best thing I could do was to try to get my mind off all the ruckus.

Running about, carrying on, it's like the little girl's Christmas bows. Her family was probably so busy they never got around to taking off the bows after Christmas. I remember back when Christmas didn't used to be that way. It was a real holiday. Years ago, everyone used to get off work for Christmas. And most people even got paid for it! It wasn't so commercial. It was a time for family and friends to get together. It was relaxed and restful, not rushed and pressured and packed full of a month's worth of headaches crammed into a single day.

And the Christmas season started about the first or second week in December. Now when I go into a store, the Christmas merchandise is up beside the Halloween candy. I remember a merchant used to run a sale they called "Christmas in July." Pretty soon, everybody will be trying to sell the Christmas merchandise in July—anything for a dollar!

Christmas was always a grand holiday. Growing up, my family always celebrated Christmas on Christmas Eve, at least after I got to be six or seven years old. When my brother and I were young, we would leave with my father in the truck and ride around. My dad had a 1968 Ford F100 he brought brand-new. It was so plain that it didn't even have a radio, but it was new. It even smelled new. I can't remember where we went, just that we rode around going nowhere in particular. After driving around for a while, we would go back home. He would make us sit in the truck, and he would holler at Mom, "Has Santa Clause been by here yet?"

They always told us that Santa Clause had been spotted in his sleigh in the area close to where we lived. As long as we were up and awake, he wouldn't come by to see us. But it just so happened that if we left, he would magically know that we weren't home and maybe, just maybe, he might stop by and leave our presents. After all, he was on a very tight schedule with a lot of good little boys and girls to go see! Every year, we somehow got lucky; he stopped by while we were out in the truck with our dad.

But that was just the first Christmas of the season. We always had Christmas several times. That was the one we considered our "big" Christmas. Our parents always got us more presents than the aunts and uncles and other people. But on Christmas night, the family would go celebrate Christmas with my mother's family. Her mother had died when all the kids were very young. That left my grandfather as a single parent, way back before that became fashionable or at least common. He was a single man trying to raise three girls by himself. It had to be hard on all of them. He was not very well educated and did not make a great deal of money. He was plenty smart enough, but growing up in the country when he did, like many folks back in his time, he ended up quitting school to work and help support the family.

They always had plenty of food to eat and a warm dry bed to crawl into at night, especially in the summer. (No one had air conditioning back in the 1930s). And no matter how tough things got, he always had enough to share with family, friends, or even strangers if they were doing without. Back then, people would take strangers into their home and feed them if they were in need. There wasn't so much concern about getting killed or raped or robbed. In fact, most people didn't even feel the need to lock their doors at night, at least not the country folks. It's gotten so bad now that someone broke into my garage and robbed me one night while I was home! I was lying in bed asleep, and they broke in anyway.

Just as my grandfather was kind to strangers, he was even more kind to us. He didn't do the shopping himself. One of his daughters, my mom or my aunt, would take him or just go do the shopping for him. He spent the same amount on each of his grandchildren. He would spend fifty or a hundred dollars each, back when that was a lot of money. We would make up a list of what we wanted from him. There was little or no improvisation; we got what was on the list. We soon learned that if there was one thing we really, really wanted to ask him for it. We would be sure to get it from him, as long as it was "tops" on our list. Our parents or someone else might decide "it would better to get a different one" or "they would rather have this other one" or "I spent so much on this other gift (probably one you didn't care about) that there wasn't enough money left to get that one thing you wanted."

There was, of course, a downside. We could be reasonably sure that we would get that one gift we really wanted, but not until Christmas night! That was the last Christmas gathering. That meant we would have to wait all of Christmas Eve and then all of Christmas day before we would finally get that one gift we were wanting so badly. Almost every year, the anticipation would just about kill me. That was the longest lasting (most years) and the most meaningful family gathering outside of the immediate family every year.

As kids, we were always focused on the presents, but over time, the holidays took on a new meaning for me. At first, it became more about family and friends, and then it gained a whole new significance. Christmas was a time, or perhaps *the* time, when the family got together every year. We always had a dinner on certain major holidays, but not everyone was there. Occasionally everyone would make it, but that was certainly the exception rather than the rule.

In college, everyone went home for Christmas. People lived in different states and were scattered everywhere during Christmas break and summer. Christmas was the one time of year when I could count on seeing all my family. During most of my college career, my brother was in law school in another state. I hardly ever saw him except when school was not in session. We were both busy. I seemed to have more going on every year. Christmas kept getting busier and increasingly more about myself and my friends, and less about giving to others. One year was different. I can't say if it was the coldness of the winter, the dampness of the season, or perhaps the hands of destiny reaching out to manipulate my life, but one particular year, I became involved in a charity drive to provide toys for needy families.

I know that many people give to the needy, especially during the holiday season. There was really nothing special about what I did. I helped raise money and awareness for a program in a local town. Children had made lists of one thing, not too expensive, they would really like to have for Christmas. Something about being involved, even in a small way, just touched my heart. These kids were so poor. I had always felt like I hadn't had that much, especially when I compared my situation to that of someone else I knew. There was always someone else with more. But seeing how little these kids had made me feel rich. They had "done without" so much for so long, that the smallest of gifts would either have them jumping up and down in ecstasy or crying in overwhelmed appreciation.

Many of them were just practical, presumably because they lacked so many of the basic necessities that we take for granted every day. Some would ask for a warm winter coat or a new pair of shoes for their Christmas present. I guess it's hard to enjoy a new toy when you're freezing. Then there was the occasional child that wouldn't ask for anything for themselves, but would instead ask for something for a brother or sister or even a parent.

The experience gave me a greater sense of appreciation for all that I had, and a greater appreciation for the true meaning of Christmas. I gained a much greater appreciation for the religious significance of Christmas when I became older. After I got married and had kids of my own, my perspective changed regarding so many things. I loved my kids so much. I had never appreciated how much my parents loved me, how much I had hurt them, how much I had disappointed them, or how much they had sacrificed until I had kids of my own and experienced all those same things from the other point of view.

Taking my son to his first football game allowed me to experience some of the sacrifice parents make for their children. We lived in Athens, Georgia. No matter what town you may think is the king of college towns, you need to be in Athens on game day before you decide. The entire city revolves around football and the university. Nearly every business in town has some type of advertisement showing their support for the Georgia Bulldogs. We weren't just going to any football game; this was a SEC conference rivalry. Emotions would be high, and the aura of that 1980 national championship was still lingering. When we walked into the stadium, it literally felt like electricity was in the air!

My son's first game was surely of sufficient magnitude to have a long-lasting impact. He was around five years old, dressed in the home team colors. I had even purchased my waist-high companion a Bulldog shirt to wear. He didn't understand the rules, but he was aware that something special was going on. His adrenalin, as well as my own, was keeping the energy level astronomical. But, by the end of the game, he was ready to crash. Unfortunately, I was not able to do likewise.

Now, you need to keep in mind that football stadiums may be designed to seat eighty or ninety thousand people, but adjacent parking lots are only designed to park about ten to twenty thousand automobiles, at most. We had parked about a mile or two away and walked. That wasn't so bad when we were excited, anticipating the game, but it seemed like forever when trying to walk back after the game. Worn out, my son just couldn't make it. I ended up having to pick him up and carry him a mile or more to get back to the car. Of course, getting back to the car after the game was uphill nearly the whole way! I was worn out, my arms and legs were worn out, and I felt completely exhausted. I wondered, *Why did I park there? Why didn't I realize he would be too tired to walk back? Why did I not anticipate any of this?* It just seemed like fate was somehow against me.

I made the sacrifice, though. Even if fate was giving me

obstacles, I was managing to overcome them. There is much that a father will do for his son!

When my son was born, we lived in a two-story house. The staircase went straight up from the entry foyer to the upstairs hallway. There was no landing or turns in the stairs at all. One afternoon, I was upstairs with my son. He was just an infant, much too young to walk or even stand up. I was carrying him in my arms down the hall. When we got to the stairway, I pivoted around the banister and started down the stairs. I was holding him with both hands, up about chin level. As I started down the stairs, a foot got caught and I tripped, falling forward. I fell from the top step all the way to the bottom of the staircase, onto the level floor. I didn't fall through the air, but down the steps. I hopped, skipped, and bounced all the way to the bottom, securely holding my son up in the air, safely, the entire time. I kept both hands on him, rather than catching myself. My instinct was not to save myself but to protect him. When we finally came to a stop, only my pride was damaged. I may have had a bruise or two, but nothing too serious. He was all smiles and laughter, safe in Daddy's arms. I guess he just figured he was on a fun ride with dear old Dad coming along!

Much like my perspective on Christmas, my way of looking at just about everything changed. I have heard that kids have that effect on people. And while I always wanted to give them more and better than I had, and more and better than even what they had, it was not until years later that I came to realize what was really important. What my parents had given me was love. Sometimes they gave me understanding, but oftentimes not. Sometimes they gave me encouragement, but other times they did not really approve and so didn't encourage me then. Sometimes they overwhelmed me with discourse, probably more than I wanted. At other times, however, they bit their tongue and turned their head to my mistakes and follies. But through it all, in everything, they always gave me love and concern. Throughout my life, I have made many mistakes. Perhaps the greatest mistake was my failure to show love at *every* moment—regardless of what might be transpiring.

$\mathscr{E}$ight

MY PARENTS WERE A LITTLE superstitious, but very much Western in their understanding of the cosmos. Energy flows and meridians in the human body were fantasy in their eyes. It was years before they would admit that a chiropractor was any more than a modern-day witch doctor. But at the same time, they firmly believed that washing your car could cause rain, and a broken mirror could cause seven years of bad luck. They weren't trying to be hypocritical; they just never reconciled all their beliefs with one another.

My mother told me the story once of something that had happened to her when she was little. She was asleep in bed. It was just an ordinary night, nothing unusual. During the middle of the night, she woke up terrified and crying. She had experienced a horrible feeling that something bad had happened to one of her family members—an aunt, I believe. She didn't understand, and she didn't know why; she just had a strong sensation, like a premonition, that some bad fate had befallen this particular member of her family. The next morning, her parents received a phone call that the family member she had been worried about had died the previous night, at precisely the same time the horrible feeling had hit her.

She was upset and very frightened. She told me that she prayed to God that she would never experience such a thing again. And, to this day, she never has. I have had those types of experiences. Mine were very different and didn't involve anyone else dying. But they were nonetheless premonitions or, at least, déjà vu experiences. The effect they had on me was to make me wonder about the world and about life.

One of the more memorable ones happened when I was a freshman in high school. The school had a dance that my older brother and I both attended. He was old enough to drive, but I was not. Well, you know what that means. As was inevitable, which I'm sure any older brother would attest to, he got stuck having to provide me with a ride. It was getting late, and the dance was nearly over. We were both still there, but I knew it was almost time to go. My brother approached me and told me to wait there for him, that he would be back in a little while. The first thing I wanted to know: "Where are you going?"

He didn't respond at first. He just told me to wait and that he would be right back. I continued to badger him until he finally told me it was none of my business. Undeterred, I continued to question him until I finally got it out of him—he was taking a friend home. *Now, why couldn't he just tell me that in the first place?* I wondered.

Of course, I wanted to tag along. And the last thing a sixteen-year-old boy wants is his fourteen-year-old kid brother tagging along! As stubborn and contrary as I always thought he was, I was even worse. Obstinate, I continued arguing and pestering him until he finally gave in. I wore him into submission.

Having finally agreed to let me go along, he instructed me to sit in the backseat and not breathe a word! I was to be as quiet and unobtrusive as possible. There were a couple more people going with us, so I was a fifth person. He had a 1967 Mercury Cougar, a sporty car back then. It was quite similar to a Ford Mustang, but a little different. It was crowded, and I had to sit in the middle of the backseat on the hump. But do you think I was complaining? I was happy just to be going along!

The "friend" he was taking home was a girl. She lived in a section of town not very far from the school where the dance was held. None of my friends lived close to where she lived, so it turned out to be a section of town with which I was completely unfamiliar. Not only had I never been to her house or down her street, I had never even been to that neighborhood before!

Eyes wide open, I was noticing everything. We pulled up to her house and into the drive. It was an older house, even back then—a white frame house, the kind built in the 1940s and 1950s. It had a porch across the front that turned down the left side of the house (if you were facing it). There was a light on the front porch. It was not mounted to a wall, nor was it a fixture attached to the porch's ceiling. It was a bulb screwed into a socket hanging down directly in front of the front door. When electricity was added to homes years ago (and maybe even in the original construction, too), light sockets sometimes dangled from the ceiling, attached by heavy electrical wires. The light bulb screwed into the socket and just hung there, with no real fixture as we generally have now.

My brother got out of the car and escorted the young lady to the front door. As soon as they reached the porch, I recognized it. I had seen this scene before—exactly. I recognized the house even though I had never been there. Then my experience went beyond typical déjà vu. Not only did I recognize the unfamiliar scene, but I knew what was about to happen! I knew the front door was about to open and a somewhat heavy woman was about to come out onto the front porch, and she did! I correctly anticipated the broad floral pattern on her blue dress. I knew where each person would go, what they would do, and even how they would look. It was as if I had already choreographed this production in my mind, and now I was just watching them act it out. The light bulb without a fixture illuminating the white front porch was correct, as was every detail of the scene. Every movement was strangely familiar and just as anticipated. Would I too experience a loved one's death as my mother had? The fear caused me to tremble as I quietly awaited my brother's return.

The effect this experience had on me was profound. Not that any new truths were revealed or mysteriously uncovered, but it led me to a radically different way of thinking. I began pondering the mysteries of the universe. "What ifs" became paramount. What if I had *not* argued with my brother about going with him? What if he had just left and not even told me that he was going? What if he had said no and stuck to it? What if I had been a little nicer and let him go without me? So many what ifs …

It was almost like I was somehow destined, or perhaps *pre*destined, to argue, to persuade, and then to go. I thought I had a certain amount of control over my own life and the decisions I was making, but now it seemed almost as if the decisions had been made for me, in advance! Was I the one on stage, acting out a life that had already been choreographed in God's mind?

Nine

"OH, GOSH, THE HEAT!" I wondered how God could have put me through this! I did not feel the cooling breeze that usually swept across the sand. Instead, I just felt heat. The sand was hot, the sun was hot, and even the air was hot. I could see the blue sky and an occasional seagull fly by. *I thought there were people here. Where could they have gone?*

My awareness of them had vanished as I slipped back inside myself. As far as I could tell, I was alone. Again.

So much of my life, I have been alone. I grew up on a farm, alone. I never seemed to develop people skills and spent my entire youth alone. I went to high school and had trouble making friends—again finding myself alone. I went to college and roomed alone. I dated, joined a fraternity, and played sports. All those relationships were superficial. No matter how many people were around, I managed to be alone!

Solitude was both a curse and a blessing. It was empty and lonely at times. There were many times when I had no one with whom to share my joys and successes. When I needed help or support, there was no one to turn to on whom I could depend. Others never seemed to understand my thoughts, my fantasies, or my ideas. Were they strange, or just too deep? Other students my age didn't seem to ponder the mysteries of the universe that so often intrigued me.

There was so much here to explore! The world seemed boundless in every direction! The more I studied and learned, the more I realized how little I actually knew. I seemed unable to discover any answers, only potentialities. There was so much potential everywhere, and so little awareness and comprehension.

After thoroughly examining all the possibilities in my head, I could still reach few, if any, verifiable conclusions. No answers were logically justified, given the facts as I knew them. More questions were raised than answers. I began to concern myself *internally* with different matters. Rather than being completely preoccupied with the typical, insignificant matters, I was taking time to ponder deeper, more meaningful questions. Of course, being able to come up with a few answers would have been nice, too!

While most of my exposure regarding philosophic investigations had come from home and church, I began to get exposure to strange new ideas. I remember a quote from Hamlet, "There are more things in heaven and earth, Horatio, than are dreamt of in your philosophy." Sure enough, I was beginning to see a world much larger and more magnificent than any I had ever imagined. I had been exposed to the occult, to Eastern thought, and to ancient philosophic perspectives as well as the more traditional, contemporary religious doctrine. Now, my contemplations went beyond resurrection, immaculate conception, and scriptural integrity. I was now considering dialectical materialism, spirituality, and existentialism.

While I found existentialism interesting, its limited focus did not satisfy my divergent interests. The limited exposure I had to the existentialist philosophy convinced me that Sartre and Nietzsche were too preoccupied with a personal interpretation of reality. To them, reality seemed to be a function of individual experience and interpretation. My own opinion had become too well grounded in traditional, objective, Western thinking to allow myself to deny the independent existence of a more universal common reality.

I struggled with the onerous question, "If a tree fell in the woods and no one was there to experience it, would it make a noise?" My teacher had insisted that it wouldn't, while in my own mind, I was convinced that it did. Eventually, I concluded that it was a matter of definition and verbiage. Does the vibration of a substance that results in sound waves necessarily produce sound irrespective of its reception? Or is "sound" defined by the occurrence of someone or something receiving the sounds waves that have been transmitted through a medium like air or water? I felt that this notion was not focused as much on philosophy as it was semantics.

Dialectical materialism didn't receive quite as much thought. It is sublimely present and discreetly introduced into your thinking when studying the martial arts. Dialectical materialism views matter as the subject of constant change caused by the opposition of the internal contradictions believed to be inherent in all things. This Marxian view is similar to yin and yang in Eastern thought.

Also called yinyang, this principle represents opposites inherent in all things. It is the dualistic nature of being both mental and physical, masculine and feminine, strong and weak, or black and white. It represents the balance of nature, harmonizing of nature, the waxing and waning of both the physical and spiritual world. This is not a philosophy in itself, but merely a principle found in many Chinese and Eastern philosophies.

Marx never used the phrase "dialectical materialism" to describe his own philosophy—that was coined later. He did take Hegel's dialectics and, in his own words, "put [it] … back on its feet." He further claimed in the Communist Manifesto in 1848 that, "the history of all hitherto existing society is the history of class struggles." Marx combined Hegel's dialectics with the notion of material class struggles to form what was later called dialectical materialism. In his view, conflict and struggle was the underlying theme and perhaps the cause of much of human history. Unlike Eastern thought, materialism played a significant role in his thinking. But I had my own interpretation of the phenomenon Marx had witnessed. People are not generally motivated by the daily desire to be middle class or upper class. The motivation today, it seems, is simply money. People want money and the things that accompany it. This is not necessarily a greedy, selfish desire. Some seek merely subsistence or a greater level of comfort. Many people will not admit to a desire for riches or wealth, but only a desire to be "comfortable." Of course, everybody has a different definition of what it takes to be comfortable. The struggle for most is not what Marx saw as a class struggle, but instead a struggle to gain more money, more things, more power, and more influence.

My philosophic ideas were further broadened and challenged in the most unusual of places. A local motorcycle dealer was doing a radio promotion with a live feed from the showroom floor. I happened to walk in and ended up talking to the person. Radio personalities are generally there for their voice alone, not their appearance. He was a slender, middle-aged man who was tidy and well kept. He did not strike me as being particularly attractive, but he was not especially unattractive, either. He just looked average, wearing blue jeans and a polo shirt. I have no idea how this came up in our conversation, but he was telling me how many angstroms wide the nucleus of some particular atom measured. I knew, by chance, because I happened to be studying that in my science class that very day. But what was his excuse? How could he possibly know that? Why would he know that?

As we talked, he asked me, "Have you ever felt like the world of thoughts and ideas might be the *real* world?"

"Well, what do you mean exactly?" I asked.

"Has it ever occurred to you that the physical world might not be what's really real? Maybe it's just a manifestation of our thoughts and ideas," he continued. "Maybe *they* are what's real!" He stepped around a new Suzuki GT380 to approach me, making his point.

"So," I said, "you think this motorcycle is a figment of my imagination? Or, perhaps, our shared imagination?" He smiled, but before he could speak, a loud noise from the intercom interrupted him. He stood dazed, trying to regain his thoughts.

Before he could continue, I confessed, "You know, at times I have imagined that when we play a football game, we never really *do* anything. I have pictured all one hundred players off both teams just sitting in a room, in folding chairs wearing street clothes, *thinking* about playing football—the opposing team's thoughts colliding with your team's thoughts. It's like we just picture the game in our minds, and we hold onto that picture so tightly that we think it's real. And other people can even see it, too! They think it's real. Could it be more like a shared vision than a physical activity?"

"Yeah! That's exactly what I'm saying!" He was getting excited by this point, clearly having regained his composure.

"Do you really believe that's true? Do you think," I asked, "that the physical world is just an illusion our minds have made up to play tricks on us?"

"No, not exactly," he answered. "I don't think our mind is trying to play tricks on us necessarily. But I do believe that thoughts and ideas are all that's truly real. We have no experience of anything that we can say is real outside what we think. You *think* you see something. We all know the power of optical illusions. You *think* you feel something. If the body can't get a message to the brain, you can't see or feel or think! How can we be sure that any of that is real? We just *think* it's real!"

He was very intelligent and very persuasive. His arguments were better than mine. But it's still hard to shrug off your whole life's worth of experience for the first new notion that comes along. His ideas were more intriguing than convincing. But here I was face-to-face with more new ideas to challenge my way of thinking. I later came to know his view as idealism. That is the philosophic notion that the physical world itself, or as it is perceived, is made up of ideas. Ideas are what's real.

I might submit to the notion that ideas are real, too. I might even say that thoughts and ideas are just as real as physical objects. There has been a lot of scientific research to support that concept. The endorphins our body produces when remembering something can be just as strong and just as plentiful as they are when we actually experience that thing we are remembering. In fact, our mind cannot always differentiate between experiencing something and remembering something; the biochemical response is the same (or at least it can be).

I have witnessed the power of positive thinking. Not just confidence, but positive thinking. I saw the mind overcome physical barriers. I saw things that were, from the point of view of all my Western thinking and education, impossible. Yet, they occurred. I remember watching a movie where a Chinese man was having open heart surgery with no anesthetic. The doctors had a sheet pulled up from his neck to block the view, where he could not see the doctors operating on him. This was also done for sanitation, they said. He was awake and alert and was clearly conversing with the doctors during the surgery. He had a series of acupuncture needles inserted to block the pain. It was hard to watch that and still claim that acupuncture was just a hoax!

Many of the claims of the Far East remain unsubstantiated. But as an increasing number of them have been documented and verified, it has become impossible for me to completely dismiss the Eastern point of view. When I read Chinese philosophy, I was intrigued to find it so similar to Christian teachings. The residents in China tend to be Buddhist, Taoist, or Confucian. The religions of Hinduism, Islam, and Christianity are present there as well. The first three were the most prevalent, though. Confucian teachings are easily meshed with Taoist teachings. The similarity of Christian teachings surprised me though. Jesus Christ and Lao Tsu both taught honor, humility, and peace. Christ said in the twenty-second and twenty-third books of Matthew, "Whoever exalts himself will be humbled, and whoever humbles himself will be exalted," and "Love the Lord your God with all your heart and with all your soul and with all your mind. This is the first and greatest commandment. And the second is like to it: Love your neighbor as yourself." Lao Tzu likewise taught similar virtues. He said, "Being deeply loved by someone gives you strength, while loving someone deeply gives you courage." They both revered the land and all of nature. They both upheld the principles of human rights and dignity. They lived and taught in very different worlds, but both maintained certain ideals reflected in their respective messages.

In my own mind, I was absorbing all the information I could. Some of it was beyond what I could really process and comprehend. But sometimes the seeds of an idea can take many years to reach fruition. I was bothered by concepts that I realized I had been unable to fully grasp. It made me feel somehow inferior to think of others' ideas existing beyond my ability to comprehend them. I continued to struggle with some, but frequently got sidetracked before I became too disappointed with myself. Perhaps it is sometimes easier to master a small task than to face the challenge of trying to master a large one.

$\mathcal{T}\!en$

THE AIR WAS HOT AND heavy. The humidity seemed unbearable. Was there no relief from this tropical broiler?

Now, science was a completely different matter! I remember sitting through endless hours of lectures. Science and physics seemed most intriguing, but many teachers and professors were excruciatingly boring. I think some teachers were not really equipped to teach science—they just got stuck having to teach it for some reason.

Studying moles and chemistry had its moments, but the most interesting part of science to me was subatomic and molecular theory. I studied under a professor of physics, Dr. Paul Hurray, who was brilliant but completely unable to teach the material selected for the class. He was a middle-aged man, average height, and a little overweight, with black hair beginning to gray. His speech was strong and deliberate, exuding experience and authority. While he was very knowledgeable and interesting, the material was so advanced that no one in the class could comprehend it. It was a freshman honors course, the only undergraduate course he taught. He devoted an entire class to dissecting Einstein's Field Theorem mathematically. It is a fifth-dimensional equation. We later spoke to graduate students in math who said they were familiar with fifth-dimensional equations, but they could not begin to work one. The idea that freshmen could comprehend this material seemed absurd. We just sat through the lecture, looking at each other, lost. I was relieved to know that others shared that same "deer in the headlights look" that I must have had. Dr. Hurray kept lecturing, seemingly oblivious to our state.

At other times, though, he thoroughly entertained us with stories of science and life. One time, he described a brilliant scientist who was working at a university. He was drafted and subsequently reported to the Selective Service board for examination, to determine his fitness for service. He was deemed physically fit but mentally unfit. A genius with outstanding intellectual credentials was not mentally competent to serve in the military?

His fascinating stories captured our attention and imagination, inspiring us. Nuclear physics and related subjects had caught my attention. I did a report on Albert Einstein and was fascinated by his life and studies.

A Jew, Einstein escaped the terror of Nazi Germany by moving to Italy, then Switzerland, and finally to the United States. His work was key in the theoretical development of nuclear physics that led to the development of the atomic bomb, which substantially enabled the United States to pressure Japan into surrender. He did not assist in developing the weapon, but he did help a relatively unknown Hungarian immigrant get the necessary resources by signing a letter to President Franklin D. Roosevelt. That immigrant, Leó Szilárd, worked with the Manhattan Project to harness nuclear fission for military purposes.

Einstein was a humanitarian. He worked for peace and justice among the world's nations. In fact, he corresponded with Sigmund Freud on their joint presentation of "What can be done to rid mankind of the menace of war." He is famous for having failed his college entrance exam. But what most people don't realize is that he took the exam at the tender age of sixteen without having finished high school. His marks (compared to high school graduates) were exemplary in mathematics and physics, but lacking in other areas, causing him to fail.

Einstein's work on light, gravity, the photoelectric effect, and electrodynamics was overshadowed by his theory of relativity and his work on a unified field theory. His general theory of relativity suggested that small amounts of matter can be converted into large amounts of energy. This suggestion was in direct opposition to the axiom holding that "matter can neither be created nor destroyed."

The theoretical justification for his assertions did not seem nearly as hard to swallow as the later mysteries of quantum physics. It also didn't interest me as much as his special theory of relativity, presented in a paper in the "Annalen der Physik" in 1905, which dealt with the electrodynamics of objects in motion. He proposed that the constant velocity of light was independent of the state of motion of its source. He introduced a space-time model that applied to a body in motion. He theorized that the space-time frame of a moving body (as its velocity approaches the speed of light) would slow down and contract in the direction of the motion, relative to a stationary observer.

I was so taken by my internal contemplation of this theory that I wrote a paper about it when I was a freshman in college, barely eighteen years old. It was for an interdisciplinary honors course called Time and the Human Experience. That course seemed like it was designed just for me. My selection of this particular university and the college's selection of course offerings seemed so improbable and yet so perfect, I couldn't help but think that the hand of destiny had somehow directed me.

The paper was developed following common sense reasoning and logic that seemed clear to me. Albert Einstein himself had admitted that his theory was logically flawed, yet he maintained that it was accurate and we would someday be able to verify its truth when our technology improved sufficiently. I never understood why everyone else failed to see the connections, the *illogic* in his theory. Were they so simple and obvious that everyone saw them and took them for granted? I even went so far as to ask other people questions to discover if they knew what I knew, or at least *what I thought I knew!* The conclusion I reached from my research was that people did not know, and the great majority of them did not care! How could others have so little interest in things that were potentially of such great importance?

Everyone knows Einstein's theory of relativity: $E=mc^2$. That was known as his "general theory." The "special theory" was related in terms of the underlying framework but was different in other ways. The special theory suggested that time was not a universal constant. Instead, Einstein theorized, time was dependent upon the observer. He assumed that inertial (relative) systems are equivalent (the Galilean transformation), but he rejected Newtonian "absolute space," which provided a unique system of reference to which everything could be compared. To Einstein, relativity implied equivalence, such that no particular inertial system and corresponding frame of reference is any more valid than any other.

Einstein additionally assumed that the velocity of light was constant and moved irrespectively of its source. In examining that hypothesis with my pre–quantum physics mind, I could not imagine the audacity of assuming that an observer affects the system by simply observing! How is that possible? It is certainly not logical, and before the popular acceptance of quantum physics and the contradictory positions it supports, it was impossible for me to understand how so many people seemed to accept the proposition put forth by Einstein.

I wondered, if I wrote a paper for school and made such an audacious, unsupportable, and unlikely claim, what was the chance that my teacher would accept it just because I assured him or her that time would eventually substantiate my proposition? Not very likely, I am sure!

But when Einstein suggested that watching something from a distance without interacting with it would somehow alter the object of your observation, the whole scientific community somehow bought into it! Rather than attacking the logic, or lack thereof, I went after the ensuing evidence that seemed to support it.

We had sent a clock into space on a rocket that traveled at a very high rate of speed. When it returned, we compared the clock in motion to that of a stationary clock on earth. (I guess scientists just ignored the fact that the earth is not really stationary. The universe is expanding, and the earth is rotating around the sun and rotating on its axis, all at the same time. Much of this was Einstein's point about relativity: relative to what? And how is being relative to any one system any better or more proper than being relative to some other system?) The clocks' time differed, just as Einstein had predicted.

But how do we know the clocks were accurate? Is time a constant or a variable? And, no matter what answer you give, I can still ask the question, "Relative to what?" Interestingly enough, the scientists had already expected and prepared for this question! The clocks used were the most accurate clocks known to man, atomic clocks. They work by using optical combs to measure (count) optical frequencies. The funny thing about clocks is that they all work in a similar way, through counting. And, the counting depends on motion.

Some clocks operate by counting the swings made by a pendulum. Some clocks operate by counting the number of vibrations of a quartz crystal. Even with an hourglass, the sand moving through is implicitly being counted or measured to determine the passage of time. A mechanical clock or a self-winding watch is dependent upon the measurement of the movement of a mechanical device. In every example of a clock, measuring time is dependent upon motion.

We measure, experience, and define time in terms of motion. Imagine being trapped in an isolated dark room with no furniture, no sound, no light, and no awareness of motion around you. Trapped in your thoughts, trapped in your own mind, you would have little corresponding data available to accurately judge the passage of time. If you experienced happy, pleasant thoughts, you might think minutes had passed when it had actually been hours. But if you were consumed with thoughts of fear and anxiety, you might think many hours had passed when it had only been a few minutes. And if you were there for days or weeks, with no system of reference, you might not have any idea how much time had passed. You might try to judge the passage of time in reference to your own body's natural cyclical processes, such as getting hungry or sleepy.

Indeed our concept of time is somehow entwined with its comparison to a static system of reference, a clock. Even a calendar is a type of clock, and clocks work through motion. We measure time and experience time through motion. Which makes more sense: when we accelerate a clock to an extraordinarily high speed, the motion of the clock affects the motion of the material being measured—e.g., the quartz, the sand, the pendulum, etc.,—or the motion of the clock affects time itself? It seems to me that "motion affects motion" is much more logical than "motion affects time."

Perhaps our ability to measure time is not quite as advanced as we would like to believe. To avoid condemning the accuracy of our clocks, we might assume that motion of an electronic transition frequency emitted by atoms is constant, irrespective of the movement of its source. I know of no proof of this, and I doubt that we really have the ability to prove it. We can always question the evidence or alleged proof by asking, "What if it were going faster? Would it still hold true then?" And scientists, such as Albert Einstein in particular, hypothesized many weird, unusual effects from traveling at or beyond the speed of light. Theoretically, we may never be able to test them (assuming certain ideas are true).

While my line of thinking seems reasonable for an eighteen-year-old kid back in the seventies, my writing, structure, and development were somewhat lacking. I failed to expound upon some of the best arguments I feebly attempted to make. It is hard, if not impossible, for us to distinguish between changes in our measurement of time and changes in time itself.

Consider this hypothetical scenario, developed from the application of his special theory: A train is moving at a very high velocity. A clock is positioned onboard the train, and another is in a stationary position nearby. The train accelerates to a velocity approaching the speed of light. This very high rate of speed is maintained for a period of time, say twenty-four hours. The clock on the ground says that the twenty-four hour timespan has elapsed, but according to the clock moving at a high rate of speed, only twenty-three hours and fifty-nine minutes have elapsed. Let's assume very accurate clocks were employed, perhaps atomic clocks. Does this prove that time slowed?

Consider a second hypothetical scenario—again, a person locked inside a dark room. With no furniture, no windows, and no doors, except for the one used to enter the room, there would be no light, no clock, and complete silence. Wouldn't that person's perception of time be tremendously affected by such an environment?

We measure time by movement. All clocks employ regular, predictable movement of some kind to measure time. The movement must be regular, ongoing, consistent, and predictable. It may be the movement of sand through an hourglass, the movement of a pendulum swinging, the movement of some other mechanical apparatus, the movement of a vibrating quartz crystal, or even the wavelengths of a caesium-133 atom. But *something* is moving!

We perceive time in much the same way we measure it. Our perception is based on the movement of something, even if it is just the movement of our thoughts flowing through our imagination. Consider the second scenario. If a person was locked in a room with no light or sound, his or her awareness of the passage of time would be dramatically affected. If my kids are stuck in the car with no television, phone, iPod,, or electronic devices they will perceive ten minutes as three or four hours! Imagine spending an extended length of time in that dark, quiet environment.

It would be difficult to judge if days had gone past or perhaps weeks. POWs experienced similar confusion when detained in an isolated environment. People alone in such a manner may use biological cycles of hunger or menstruation, for example, to attempt to keep track of the passage of time.

Clocks determine time by objective measurement, though, rather than by subjective judgment. So how would an unbiased clock be influenced by the rate of motion? Remember that all clocks depend upon the regular, ongoing, consistent, and predictable movement of something. The passage of time is assumed to be consistent and equivalent, relative to the movement of whatever device is employed by the clock. The relative systems are considered equivalent, such that their relationship is fixed or static. If their relationship is dynamic, then one could not accurately predict the passage of time based on the relative movement to which it is being associated.

To clarify this, consider the first scenario again. Imagine that the two clocks in this experiment use a swinging pendulum to measure the passage of time. The stationary clock's pendulum swings in the normal, ordinary, expected manner. But the force of acceleration interferes with the motion of the pendulum swinging on the clock moving in the train. This influences the way it swings, perhaps altering the length of its arc or the rapidity. It isn't hard to imagine a pendulum being affected.

If its movement could be altered, why not the movement of vibrating quartz or perhaps the wavelengths measured in an atomic clock?

The idea that movement affects time is extraordinary, but the idea that movement could affect movement (of a pendulum, for example) seems quite easy to believe. Perhaps our so-called scientific proof really shows that movement affects our clock's ability to measure time accurately.

Even beyond this problem lies a greater inconsistency. It seems to push the underlying postulates of relativity toward an incompatible hypocrisy. Relativity is designed to relate two or more inertial systems, relative to each other. We examine one as stationary and the other moving at a high relative rate of speed. No one inertial system is considered any better or more valid than any other. How can one ever be stationary, since position is by definition a relative term? With the universe expanding, the earth spinning, and the solar system moving, changing its position within the Milky Way galaxy, how could anything or any system ever be stationary? The term "stationary" places something's location about as precisely as the term "infinity."

The concept of a fixed, stationary position, in absolute terms, is a practical if not theoretical impossibility. Movement, or lack thereof, only exists in relative terms. Something appears to be stationary if you are located in the same frame of reference as the item in question. In that case, the item is certainly not stationary in absolute terms, but is stationary in relative terms— e.g., relative to your position that is likewise "fixed" within the same frame of reference.

Mathematically, Einstein used equations that were algebraically inconsistent, disregarding initial constraints and then manipulating his resulting equation by γ to correct the inconsistency. He theorized distortions of time and space caused by motion. He postulated characteristics of particles and assigned those traits to light. Then he theorized that light's characteristics apply to material objects. In this way, he argued that acceleration of an object beyond the speed of light is impossible. Of course, using similar logic, Zeno also "proved" that Achilles was unable to catch and overtake a tortoise.

Civilization thought that science provided reasonable explanations for observed phenomenon. Then along came greater advancement with theories, such as relativity, that seemed to demonstrate the old science's inability to formulate plausible explanations for certain things. The new science of relativity seemed to resolve some of the issues that had been so puzzling to scientists. Then as we learned more, we discovered that the new science also had shortcomings that remained unexplainable. We developed another new science of quantum physics that seems to better explain certain occurrences. I suspect that as we learn more and develop even more powerful technology, we will learn that quantum physics is wrong (or at least limited) in its ability to deal with some things, just as relativistic physics is. Sometimes it seems like the more we learn, the less we know. But I guess it would be more accurate to say the more we learn, the more we see how little we know. Science may be the epitome of what we know. I just felt bad for not having contributed to the big universe of "what we know!"

Eleven

I FELT SOMETHING CRAWL ACROSS MY hand. It briefly brought back my awareness to the sand, sun, and heat. It didn't exactly itch … or tickle. It was a little irritating, but not enough to spur me to action. It came and was gone, much like we, as people, do. We come here to experience life in this shell we call a body, and then we die and fade away and are forgotten. *Here I am lying in the sun, scorching from its heat … We all lie in the sun like this. Some people bask in the sun, while others wilt and perspire from its intensity. What shall I do? Bask or wilt?*

The heat and my age incline me to wilt. That would be the natural, scientific reaction, wouldn't it? The heat saps your strength, but even more than that, it saps your will! Lying in that heat, drawn to and intensified by the sand and the water, it seemed like an impossibility to overcome such obstacles! Surely, those odds were overwhelming!

When I considered the temperature, the dehydration, the humidity, and the weakness of so many years of hard work, how could I possibly persevere? My body's cell could not store enough nutrients. The oxygen level had become too low. It wasn't physically possible! Physiology was against me; science was against me!

I had always been fond of science—until then! Sure, there were parts that were boring to me, but dissecting a frog has a certain appeal to a fourteen-year-old boy. As we examine science, we find that the art of science has its own rules and peculiarities. Some seem very reasonable, while others seem arbitrary or even obstinate. Sometimes the task of reconciling science with the rest of life seems quite daunting.

Science teaches us the scientific method. This scientific method provides an established methodology for attacking a question or problem in the appropriate, scholarly manner. We find, however, that life does not always conform to the idioms of science, or of the scientific method. The culture adopted in science has become so pervasive in Western society that we have even developed the saying, "seeing is believing."

What about the things we can't see? We have stubbornly clung to our acknowledgment of love, even though we cannot see, hear, or touch it. Yet many notions, equally real but similarly abstract, have been disregarded as fantasy, legend, or superstition. We have developed theories and devoted countless hours of study to the task of legitimizing abstract concepts such as fear, love, anxiety, and doubt. We seem to need to give ourselves a rational, intellectual justification for accepting these concepts, so we attempt to study and explain them. But human emotional responses are so personal and individual that categorization and explanation is evasive, at best.

How could you explain fear to someone who has never been afraid? How could you explain love to someone who has never felt it? At the same time, each of us has a unique perspective and experience of each of these emotions. While most of us share common traits that characterize a particular emotion, our specific emotional response remains highly individual.

And while we can accept the existence of emotions, something we feel and experience firsthand, we find it much more difficult to accept the existence of hell, ghosts, angels, witchcraft, magic, soul travel, demon possession, and divination. These, and many more similar things, are much more accepted in other cultures where modern science has not bred so much skepticism. We typically call those cultures "backward" and "superstitious." But as proof emerges to justify the supernatural, skeptics assault the supporters of such claims with charges of fraud, exaggeration, and sensationalism.

While these charges have been true in some cases, there remain a number of instances where no such claims can be substantiated. There remains just as much proof that angels do exist as proof that they do not. So, inevitably, man believes what he chooses to believe. We accept that which we want to believe and reject that which we don't.

Science provides us with the rationale for examining circumstances from a completely objective point of view. But what do we do when our objective evaluations cannot satisfactorily explain observed phenomenon? Some realities defy explanation. Some explanations may never be captured or understood/comprehended. Science is limited by our knowledge, experience, and imagination.

Quantum physics, for example, challenges much of what we know, or *thought we knew*, about the universe. We observe "something" and cannot determine certain aspects of its nature. Quantum superposition suggests that an object can be in more than one place at the same time. The simple act of observing that object relegates it to a single location, but how can simply looking at something change its location? Or limit its location?

The simple act of observing can cause the object of that observation to quit behaving like a wave and start behaving like a particle. Is it a particle or is it a wave? How can a detached, uninvolved observer alter the nature and/or characteristics of the object?

There have been many claims of telekinesis—that is, using your mind to exact a physical change in something. Some have been discredited, while others remain apparently valid. In an experiment, there was an attempt to lower the violent crime rate in Washington DC by utilizing mind power. Based on similar past experiences, the goal of a 15 percent reduction in violent crime was targeted. When the chief of police was consulted, he said it would take an act of God to reduce the violent crime rate by that amount. It had not been that low in over twenty years!

To affect this change, a number of spiritual leaders of various beliefs and cultures were collected at the nation's capital. They meditated, prayed, and chanted, around the clock, for six weeks. During that period of time, this group focused its thoughts and attention on peace, with a resultant reduction in violent crime. The violent crime rate was actually reduced by 18 percent. That may seem like an anomaly, but other independent attempts to do the same thing yielded similar results.

In an experiment done by Dr. Masaru Emoto in Japan, distilled water was placed in glass jars. He purposefully fixed his thought, his intentions, on the water in the jars. He labeled each jar with the thought or intention he held toward that jar's water. He bombarded the jar and its contents with a specific idea. Though Dr. Emoto claims no special mental powers or abilities, he used thought and intention to transform the crystalline structure and nature of the water molecules themselves. Whether this change was manifested by the power of intention, by pure thought, or by simply positive (or negative) energy is still in question. But the amazing transformation has far-reaching implications that transcend the realm of modern science and defy rational, scientific explanation.

When you consider the necessary role water plays in supporting life, the power of water is staggering. Water, through erosion, can literally move mountains. Water, through weather, can devastate huge areas, leaving little unscathed. Water is the building block of life, and little could survive without it. Our bodies are more than 60 percent water. Water we drink cleanses our bodies and flushes out toxins. It hydrates cells and allows chemical processes within our bodies to occur. Water washes us and cleans cuts and wounds. Water cleanses and purifies. And just imagine how susceptible water is to the influence of this energy! Even without perfect understanding, we can positively identify ourselves as the source of this energy. Maybe it's our aura, our chi, our intention, or our simply spirit reaching out, but whatever the specifics, it still remains an energy originating inside of each of us. This energy is largely untapped, or at least undirected, by the vast masses that remain unaware. Perhaps we are all using it every day, with every thought, without even acknowledging its presence or power.

Think of all the different groups advocating some form of positive thinking. There are countless books on the subject. I have printed material from the 1970s outlining how to structure your workout (weight training) for maximum results. This guide spends considerable time emphasizing the importance of thinking in the correct manner. The person is instructed to imagine the muscles growing. Try to feel the muscle working. As you work the muscle, try to feel the muscle expanding and getting bigger. Hold a picture in your mind of the muscle growing and becoming huge. You are subtly instructed to employ mental exercise and discipline along with the physical exercise to obtain maximum results. Even back in the seventies, people recognized the positive influence obtainable by proper thinking. *Think and Grow Rich* is a perfect example of a book that epitomizes that view.

Friedrich Nietzsche said, "A thought, even a possibility, can shatter and transform us." Or, as Anthony Robbins said, "Beliefs have the power to create and the power to destroy." The idea that what we hold within us contains substantial power seems to be commonly held. As Peace Pilgrim said, "If you realized how powerful your thoughts are, you would never [again] think a negative thought."

The medical and scientific community still argues over the specifics of how positive thinking affects change, but the inescapable conclusion that it *does* matter still persists—even as far back as the writings of King Solomon (arguably one of the wisest kings who ever lived) who wrote, "For as a man thinketh within himself, so is he."

For thousands of years, people have recognized the importance of positive thinking, the importance of believing. Science cannot definitively explain how or why, but believing is a crucial element in success, despite any inadequacies of science to explain why!

I wonder if that would be enough. I wonder if it would work for me.

I felt something on my hand again. This time it was more irritating than before, tickling me. I could feel it laughing at me, daring me to respond. It must have sensed my helplessness. I summoned all my strength, all my positive energy, and all my determination to move my hand and rid myself of this pest. If my hand moved at all, it was slight, practically imperceptible, but the bug flew away. I felt like I had willed it into flying away, and that was sufficient.

Twelve

WHY NOT? ISN'T THAT QUERY every bit as valid as the much more commonly asked, "Why?" James Allen said, "For true success ask yourself these four questions: Why? Why not? Why not me? Why not now?"

I ask myself those now. Why? Why have I traveled down this road? Why am I here now? And, what does it all mean? So much water has passed under the bridge ... I have stumbled through life often unaware, and when I was vaguely aware, the sensation overwhelmed me. It seems ironic that I feel so dedicated to the proposition that man's ability is almost limitless, yet I have spent my life powerless to accomplish any of that which I most desired to do.

In sports, I settled for mediocrity. I did not follow the academic roads that had interested me. I worked at a dozen jobs and lost them all when the economy got tough. I have been through so much, and yet I have hardly lived at all. I wish I had spent less time dreaming and more time doing! Life is but an endless succession of opportunities, of possibilities. We can choose one and shape our destiny, or we can contemplate while the choice passes us by—vanishing forever into a future we will never know. "Not to choose" is a choice in itself. Hesitancy and doubt paralyze us as we stare into our own future. The timid are left behind while the aggressive charge forward! I, too, have been aggressive—making extemporaneous decisions without fully recognizing the results. My hurried decisions haunted me, while my carefully calculated ones were often just as bad.

I remember my uncle telling me when we played checkers, "Study long, study wrong!" Often, it really didn't seem to matter. I made bad decisions for all the wrong reasons. I passed up good jobs I could have secured because the application process was too drawn out and difficult. Times when I ought to have taken the easy way out, I didn't. Instead, I wasted countless hours performing a meaningless task, accomplishing no real purpose.

Then, at other times, I did take the easy way out when I shouldn't have. Full of doubt and skepticism, I wasted much of my youth. Lonely and remorseful, I wasted much of my adulthood. Regrets abound, and recollecting them serves no useful purpose. Instead of looking back, I ought to have been looking ahead, or at least looking down!

As I sat in contemplation, paralyzed by the fear that I could never undo so many mistakes, I realized that I was not alone. The beach was crowded, but no one had been with me. I came by myself and had been by myself the whole time, or so I thought. Finally becoming aware of the people around me, I felt their stares and their concern. They were talking, but their words were not clear. Were they talking to me or to each other?

A stranger I hadn't noticed was sitting there beside me. His face was warm and gentle. A sort of kindness exuded from his eyes. I didn't recognize him, yet I had the strangest feeling I had known him all my life. His long flowing hair was dark brown and smooth. His skin was tan—no, make that olive—and his features looked smooth and gentle, yet aristocratic. He had an air of peace and love that almost radiated from his face.

I moved to lift a hand to the stranger, but nothing happened. It was as if I was paralyzed. My mind was awake, but my body was asleep! I pressed on, trying to lift my hand. I thought a warm gesture to welcome him would be fitting. Perhaps I looked strained, or maybe he just felt my intention, but he seemed to know what I was trying to do.

"It's all right," he reassured me. "Everything is fine. Just the way it is supposed to be."

"What do you mean, 'the way it is supposed to be'? I fell, and now I can't even move my arm!" I guess he could tell I was a little exasperated.

"It's all right," he repeated. There was a sense of finality in his voice.

"I can't seem to get up," I told him. "In fact, I don't think I can even move!"

"It's your time to rest," he told me.

I was instantly petrified. Rest? Me, rest? What was he talking about? Since when did I ever rest? When he looked at me, it was as though he could see right through me. When he started to speak, it was as if he heard my words even though I hadn't said them. Not out loud! How could he hear my thoughts?

"We all need rest sometimes," he assured me. "You have put your time in—lots of it. Now it's your time to rest."

He spoke authoritatively, but he wasn't saying what I wanted to hear. "I'm not ready to rest," I told him. "I've got places to go and things to do!"

"You have already done your part," he stated firmly. Yet, even with his firmness came a love and sympathy to which I had not been accustomed.

I stared at him. For probably the first time in my life, I was speechless. I was thinking, *Surely I'm not dead. How could I be dead? It wasn't that bad a fall, and the sand is soft ... kind of. I'm in good health. There's nothing wrong with me—or at least nothing major. I can't be dead!*

Then he spoke up, reassuringly, "You have lived a full life. You have fulfilled your purpose. Your work here is done, and it's time to move on."

"I can't move on. I've messed so much stuff up. I wasted so much time. I haven't told anyone good-bye. I haven't made any preparations."

"Sometimes we don't get to do those things," he told me.

"But I can't go. I've got to take care of my sister. She's alone, with no family and no one to take care of her. And what about my kids? I have to talk to them—to tell them ... They've got to know!" I cried out.

I must have looked sad. I mostly felt panicky. This time, he didn't respond, he didn't argue, and he didn't tell me "no." I sensed that maybe something I had just said had made a difference.

"I have to talk to my kids and everybody. They've got to know!"

"Know what, exactly?"

Was he testing me or just questioning me for information?

"They have to be warned," I blurted out (at least in my mind). "I have to let them know, so they don't make the same mistakes I made." I felt desperate. Was he listening? Was my argument convincing him of anything? I felt obliged to continue.

"I was given so much. I had some talent. Maybe I couldn't sing, and I was never a great ball player, but I was given so many other talents. I had every opportunity in the world to utilize that talent to make a difference. I coulda, shoulda used it to change lives! I could have turned somebody's life around! Who knows? Maybe a lot of people's lives. But I didn't do it; I procrastinated. And now look at me! A lot of good that talent did me!"

Then I paused. I was letting that soak in. "They've got talent, too. That's why I have to warn them—so their lives don't get wasted like mine!"

But then, after some silence (I'm not sure how much, but it seemed like forever!), the stranger finally responded. "You had a whole lifetime to make a difference. You should have done it then."

My head dropped. "I know." What else could I say? "But I promise. Give me one more chance—just a little more time— and this time I will make that difference!"

"You've already had your chance—a lifetime of chances," he told me. "If you didn't do it then, why should I believe that you will really do it now?"

A fair question, but I wasn't about to admit it! "Because now *I know*. I understand. You know, you never see it coming. No one ever expects to die. But now I realize how short life really is, how little time we really have, and now I understand the urgency!"

"If I give you one more opportunity, you had better make the most of it." He seemed most serious.

"I will. I promise. I will let everyone know." He looked

hard at me, like he was peering deep into my soul. I think he knew my sincerity. He didn't speak a word but still somehow conveyed to me that he would relent. After he had reluctantly agreed, I felt like sighing in relief. I think I really did sigh, but then I got all choked up and started gagging and coughing.

Someone grabbed my hand and put their other hand around behind me to support my back. It was a paramedic who had apparently responded to a call. The paramedic gently laid me back down. Then, turning me, I was moved into a position to make my breathing easier. After a few minutes, the coughing had stopped. I was breathing again, almost normally.

"I thought you were a goner," I heard one man say.

"Yeah, he scared me half to death," said the young girl beside him. They were both bent over me inquisitively.

"Okay. Back up and give us some room!" I suddenly noticed more paramedics around me. I had only seen one before, but now I could count at least three.

"Those uniforms sure look hot," I said. I was thinking it; I really hadn't meant to say it out loud. It just slipped out.

"Oh, we're fine," one of them responded. "Yeah, we were just worried about you! What happened?" another asked.

"I don't really know," I stammered. "I just fell."

"Well at least you're all right now. Do you hurt anywhere?" she asked me.

I had to think about that. It was as if I had forgotten to hurt! "Well," I replied cautiously, "I don't know. I think I'm okay."

"Do you think you can get up?"

"I'm not sure, but I'd like to try." They grabbed both arms and supported me under my elbows. I don't think I did much to help stand myself up; I think they just basically lifted me. But, at any rate, I was up. Not very steady, but up nonetheless.

They assisted me back off the beach to the hotel, where I could sit down in one of the chairs lining the deck around the pool. They practically had to carry me back.

"Are you going to be okay? Can we call someone for you? Can we get you anything?" they asked.

"No," I insisted. "I'll call my daughter." I said it with authority so they would believe me. When I pulled out my phone, they looked more or less convinced. As I rested and held my phone, they were greeted by a person from the hotel.

They talked and walked away. They were obviously talking about me, but I didn't care. I had one more chance—one more opportunity, even more miraculous than any of the previous ones. Right now, I just needed to rest a minute and gather myself. I had a job to do, and I was about to do it!

After talking and looking some more, they walked back over to me and checked on me one final time before departing. *Finally! I thought they'd never leave!* With a little help from one of the hotel's staff, I made my way back up to my room. She ordered some food for me before she left. I had become quite hungry from all the exertion.

I couldn't wait on the food, though. I pulled out my laptop and got to work. I knew what I had to do. It wasn't enough just to talk to my daughter and my son and to warn them. I had made a promise—a promise that I knew I would be held to, required to answer for if I failed to keep my word. Warning just my immediate family would not be sufficient. No, I had to warn everybody!

So, I sat at my computer and began to type: "As the sun beat down, I pressed onward, but not without pausing to take it all in."

Epilogue

WITHIN ALL OF US LIES the power to change and the power to make a change. We can make a change not only in ourselves, but also in our lives, our circumstances, and our world. We find ourselves handcuffed by mediocrity, suffocated by the certainty of repetition and convention. We must break out of our comfort zones and challenge ourselves to experience life and, yes, to make a difference.

We are here but for a moment. Our existence is brief and fleeting. Before we realize it, our life has vanished. We become old, and without the vigor of our youth, we lack the energy for the rigorous pursuits we imagined ourselves chasing. Tired and spent, we fall asleep for the last time unprepared. Not having accomplished the work to which we had aspired, we realize as our very existence begins to vanish before our eyes that we have failed. We have failed ourselves, failed our family, failed mankind, and even failed God. Regretting the mistakes of our past, we long to undo them.

Perhaps we can't undo the past, but how wonderful it would be to at least warn people to live! Live each day without regret! Live each day as though it were your last! Live each day having made a difference. Making a difference in someone else's life will surely make a difference in your own life as well.

Love others fully. See the beauty and majesty in all of creation. Try to open your mind and your heart to absorb all the wonder that surrounds you. Soak it all in. Love and honor and cherish the small things as much as the great ones. Live in humility and gratitude for everything. Be thankful for your parents and your children. Be thankful for your school, your country, and your job. Try not to take for granted those little blessings like running water, plumbing, and electricity, not to mention freedom. Be grateful, not just for the blessings but for the bumps in the road as well. Adversity strengthens us and builds character. It gives us the tools to overcome the future obstacles for which we otherwise would not have been prepared.

By loving and giving and helping, we can hopefully leave the world a better place than we found it, at least in our own little corner. But don't wait. The time for action is now. You never know when it will be too late!